IN HER SISTER'S SHADOW

Jim Campbell

IN HER SISTER'S SHADOW

ISBN: 978-0-615-36021-8

Published by

JaMar Publishing

6635 Baptist Valley Rd.
North Tazewell, VA 24630

Tel: 276 988-9504
Fax: 276 979-1628

E-mail jtcampsr@netscope.net
Web: www.jamescampbellbooks.com

Other books by James Campbell

Luther's Mule

Ida Mae: Moonshine, Money & Misery

INTRODUCTION

Mary Sue sat alone in the upstairs bedroom she once shared with her older sister, Ida Mae Duncan. Her elbows rested on the sill of an open window, and she cradled her chin in the palms of her hands. From where she sat, she could observe almost anything that was taking place on the Baxter farm where she and her family lived. It provided her full view of the long winding lane leading from their two-story farmhouse down through a large pasture field. At the end of the lane was the graveled road that ran along the southern boundary of the 140-acre farm. Since their home was located near the tree line, most everything that went on took place in front of their house. The rolling fields of hay, corn and tobacco lay on either side of the large pasture field. The quarter-acre garden that furnished most of her family's food supply was situated just above their springhouse below the yard fence.

Mary Sue spent hours sitting in front of her bedroom window remembering all the good times she and her sister had shared before Ida Mae married and left home. She missed those days and looked forward to future days when they could share more good times together. Those times were beginning to get closer. When she graduates from high school, she will be moving to North Carolina to live with her sister while attending college.

1

COUNTY UNREST

After the heated sheriff election in the county was over and the biggest illegal whiskey runner was buried, one would think everything would return to normal. Not the case with the folks living in the hills of Southwest Virginia. The happenings of the last few weeks did little more than start the local rumor mill grinding. Seems everyone had a different version of the events leading up to the death of Sheriff Baxter's opponent Mike Fletcher, but they all involved the Duncan Family.

There were those good religious souls who were glad the flow of moonshine through the community had come to a halt; those who pretended to be when in the presence of those afore mentioned and others, friends of the late Mike Fletcher, who vowed to get even with the parties who had caused his untimely death.

Times were hard during the years following World War II. Jobs were scarce and labor was cheap, but making whiskey was very profitable—if one knew how to follow the recipes handed down by the masters of the trade. And Masters they were. When it came to taste testing (which was most often done during horse-trading events), the old timers from the hills of Southwest Virginia were eons ahead of whoever came in second. More times than not the horse traders went home with the same animals they came with but their saddlebags were rarely empty. Few could resist the urge to take with them at least enough of the home brew for the next occasion to celebrate, usually the following weekend.

While seeking the position of sheriff, William Baxter managed to cut off the primary pipeline that furnished the flow of whiskey from the hollows of Russell and Buchanan County into North Carolina and Eastern Kentucky. This angered many of the distillers, transporters and retailers. A few were content to suffer their loss, but some were determined to seek revenge.

Ira Duncan, recently appointed chief deputy, sharecropped the farm belonging to the newly elected sheriff. He and his wife Mary Ellen (former girlfriend of the sheriff), daughter Mary Sue, sons John Robert and their thirteen-year-old twin boys Kervin and Kevin called the sheriff's farm home. Ira's cantankerous widowed mother, whom everyone called "Granny," also lived with the Duncan family.

Their oldest daughter, Ida Mae, had recently married for the second time and moved to North Carolina. Her ambition to overcome poverty and leave the farm accidentally got her involved with those who found it less strenuous to run white lightning than to be counted among the everyday work force. As it were, the episodes brought about by the actions of Ida Mae would furnish fuel for the gossip flame and haunt her family far into the future. Being closely sheltered, as most young girls were during the fifties, and being one of the most beautiful young ladies in Russell County was enough to make Ida Mae yearn for a more exciting life than furnished by local events in her surroundings.

In recent weeks she had become interested in the young deacon, Donald Hale, who accompanied the Preacher Kyle on his visit to their home each Saturday evening. Deacon Dooley, as most folks began calling him, was a tall good-looking single man in his mid-twenties who until recently was known only for his ability to beat all competition in the local pool hall. Being convinced by Preacher Kyle that gambling at this establishment would surely bring future disaster, now and in the hereafter, Donald eventually joined the Baptist Church. In a few short weeks he had made such an impression on the congregation they appointed him deacon and elected him treasurer.

Shortly after her high school graduation, Ida Mae and the deacon began dating. In a few short weeks they married. The ceremony had been planned for a later time but the sudden realization that parenthood was in their immediate future created the need for an earlier wedding day. Little did the deacon know that his involvement with Ida Mae would lead to his fall from grace. In her haste to begin what she anticipated to be a life of adventure, his new bride persuaded him to do things unfitting for someone in his position.

The newlyweds moved into a small apartment in town and the deacon spent his days at his job at a local service station. He was content with his role as a husband and looked forward to his evenings with his new bride. He didn't mind there was no money to buy the much needed furniture or decorations for the barren walls.

Ida Mae, on the other hand, soon became bored sitting in the cramped apartment waiting for the man she married to come home smelling like burned motor oil. She was excited about the arrival of their baby, but she suffered a miscarriage. This loss made her miss her family and life on the farm even more. She missed helping her mother with the everyday household chores, watching her brother John Robert tend the fields, and the twins always getting into some mischief. She even missed Granny who was constantly finding something to complain about.

In only a few short weeks, Ida Mae realized her life of adventure had rapidly become a life of boredom. After days of heated arguments, she persuaded Dooley to exercise his expertise at the billiard tables to earn extra money they needed to purchase things she craved. She convinced him to secretly take a small loan from the church treasury to begin financing his old habit. After losing all the church money, they resorted to running moonshine, which proved to be even more devastating. These escapades eventually led to the deacon's downfall, and the end of their short marriage. Before she reached the age of nineteen, she had married, divorced, and had fallen in love again.

"Not a way of life for me," Mary Sue pondered as she sat on the edge of a large boulder situated just below the overflow of a spring on Sheriff Baxter's farm. A huge weeping willow hovered over the springhouse causing her family's only water supply to stay refreshingly cool even during the hottest days of summer. This was her favorite place to hang out and reflect on happier days when her sister Ida Mae was still home. It was a place of solitude while daydreaming about her future.

Today she was really caught up in the fantasy world she imagined she would live in someday. She leaned against the trunk of the willow tree and let her bare feet dangle just barely below the surface of the water. The smell of freshly churned buttermilk cooling in the spring water and the aroma of newly sprouting peppermint only enhanced her ability to daydream.

From where she sat she could see her twin brothers swinging on the grapevines on the hillside at the edge of the woods some distance above their home. The graveled road, a short distance away, ran along the southern boundary of the Baxter farm. The sound of an occasional passing vehicle or a cloud of dust that erupted when one passed often bounced her back into reality. She would be graduating from high school in another year, and her plans were to find a way to attend college and someday become a successful lawyer.

Having grown up in the mountains where illegal whiskey ran rampant and living on a farm that belonged to the sheriff of the county, she soon learned that the need for good attorneys was in great demand. It seemed evident that the attorneys defending the bootleggers made far more money than the law enforcement officers who brought them to court. And money was what Mary Sue wanted most. She had never been further than fifty miles from her birthplace, but her longing to see the world she often read about would surely require lots of cash.

Unlike her older sister who had become infatuated with the deacon and could hardly wait to be old enough to be allowed to date, Mary Sue vowed she would do things much differently. Although she shared Ida Mae's dreams of someday leaving the life of poverty to which they had become accustomed, she was too independent to be swayed by the first man who showed interest in becoming her suitor.

She, like Ida Mae, was not allowed to keep company with anyone of the opposite sex, unless chaperoned, until she reached her eighteenth birthday. In a few weeks she would begin her senior year in high school. After graduation she could spend the summer in Winston Salem, North Carolina with Ida Mae and her new husband, Jake, one of the best billiard shots in the Southeast. With their help, she hoped to find a job that would allow her to earn enough money to enroll in college.

For months she had been dreaming of all the nice restaurants and shopping places her sister mentioned in letters. She could hardly wait to walk the streets of the big city with Ida Mae. She wanted to window shop for the beautiful dresses, high-heel shoes and expensive jewelry she had only seen in magazines.

The warm evening sun was beginning to settle behind the western peaks near their old farmhouse. Before she realized it, she had allowed herself to spend most of the afternoon in her own little dream world.

As she came back to reality she became aware of several small minnows darting playfully near her feet. A small hawk sat motionless on one of the low hanging willow tree limbs staring directly at the small creatures. "Come a little closer to the surface and I will have you for dinner," Mary Sue imagined the small bird must have been thinking.

She was completely unaware that a small water snake lurking nearby also had its eyes on the small fish. She suddenly became aware, however, when the serpent slithered across her legs and fell into the water inches from her feet. Panic stricken she let out a blood-curdling scream while kicking both feet into the air. The serpent landed several feet from where she was sitting.

In her excitement she had not noticed an automobile had come to a stop at the edge of the road near the springhouse. It was a new, shiny, green 1953 Dodge.

The driver was leaning out the window smiling from ear to ear so she gathered he must have seen what she had done.

"I lived in the mountains most of my life but that is the first time I ever saw a flying snake," he said.

"I suppose I did look rather silly," she admitted.

"Is this the Baxter farm?" the stranger asked.

"Sure is."

"Then you must be Ida Mae's little sister. My name is Jimmy Doug Hurd, but my friends call me J.D., I'm Jake's brother. I have just moved back home from Chicago and I'm reacquainting myself with the territory. I'm on my way to the Carolinas to visit some of our relatives before settling down to start helping Daddy run his business."

Mary Sue strolled to the edge of the road and reached through the wire fence to shake hands with the stranger. "Pleased to meet you J.D., my name is Mary Sue. What type of business is your father in?"

"Not at liberty to say at the moment, but Dad has informed me that due to recently changing circumstances, he may be able to earn enough money to afford a better lifestyle."

"Won't you come in and meet some other members of the family?" she invited.

"Another time, thanks. I plan to get to Winston Salem before sundown so I guess I better be moving on. I was almost sure this was the Baxter farm; and when I realized you must be Ida Mae's little sister, I thought I should stop and introduce myself. Jake and I will stop back by in a few days."

"Now ain't this one for the record books," Mary Sue thought as she watched the Dodge pull away. 'Our landlord is the county sheriff, my daddy is his chief deputy and my big sister has married into a family of newly organized moonshine runners."

She was unsure if J.D. was in fact about to get involved with the illegal whiskey business, or if she was letting her imagination run wild. She convinced herself it wasn't a matter she needed to be worried about. Baxter would rapidly put a stop to any flow of illegal brew through Russell County. After all that was how he had got himself elected. And she was sure Jake would have nothing to do with such shenanigans; her big sister would see to that.

She would mention this incident to her daddy later; right now the aroma of fresh baked cornbread and turnip greens had her full attention. She was sure not to be late for the evening meal because immediately after, her favorite country music program, *The Hillbilly Hit Parade* came on the local radio station. Most days the entire family would retire to the front porch after supper and she was left to enjoy the *Parade* while she cleaned the kitchen.

Suppertime was her mother's favorite time of day. She insisted that members of the family be present at the supper table unless some emergency demanded their presence elsewhere. It was a time for each to share the happenings of the day, make plans for tomorrow and to catch up on any community gossip.

The gossip segment was Granny's favorite time. Mary Ellen proclaimed the gossip did more good for her than the food. And now that her son had been appointed Sheriff Baxter's Chief Deputy, she had become the most interesting member of their weekly quilting bee. She tried to grasp every word Ira told the family about the illegal goings on in the county and was more than anxious to share the news with the other ladies in the group. Although her hearing was far less than perfect, she almost always got it right.

The sheriff was not one of Granny's favorite people to say the least. He was the family's landlord but he was also her daughter-in-law's old boyfriend. Therefore, if the sheriff did something a little shady, Granny was sure to get the word out at her next quilting party; but if he did something heroic, she most always forgot to mention the incident. She would have preferred not to live with her son and his family; but with no means of self-support, she had no other choice. "Just living here temporarily until some rich feller comes along and carries me away," she always says.

"When cows fly," was Mary Ellen's reply, under her breath of course.

Anyway, today was special. It was Friday evening, the supper dishes were done, and *The Hillbilly Hit Parade* had just signed off. Mary Sue was always glad when supper was over and everyone left her alone in the kitchen. Then she would turn the radio up loud and sing along with every song the D. J. played.

This evening, as most evenings in the past she joined her family on the front porch to enjoy the last rays of the autumn sunset. Along with the cool chill of the season came a premonition that all was not well. Her mother sat in the swing she normally shared with her daddy waiting for him to come home. The worried look on her face made evident her concern for his safety. John Robert sat at the top of the steps whittling on a small piece of cedar, but Mary Sue did not miss his constant glances down the lane. Even the twins who would normally be off somewhere taking advantage of the last hour of daylight sat quietly waiting for their daddy.

Ira had never been this late before. He was usually home before the evening meal was over but the incidents of the last few days demanded much more of his time. The flow of illegal whiskey through the county had become as rampant as before Sheriff Baxter was elected.

Rumor had it that some of the former sheriff's old friends were bragging that they would not be as easily caught as Fletcher had been. They made no secret about the fact they could outsmart the new sheriff and his badge-toting farmer deputies. Someone had gone so far as to place a note on Baxter's windshield, which read, "Your good ole boys might know how to punch cows but our guys know how to punch cars."

These insinuations infuriated Baxter. Maybe a couple of his deputies had been farmers but they had been able to bring down Fletcher and he vowed he would also deal with the new group of outlaws. He was so angry he had the note published in the county newspaper along with his own response. "Wait and see who gets the last PUNCH!"

It was no secret that several fast-running out-of-state automobiles with loud mufflers were now traveling through the area. Most moved late at night, some as decoys but law enforcement officers had no doubt some were transporting shine.

"Pretty soon the sheriff will chase down all those bootleggers and then Daddy and the other deputies won't have to work so late." It was Mary Sue's effort to set her family's minds at ease and relieve the tension that filled the air.

"If the old son-of-a-gun was as interested in chasing those moonshiners as he has been chasing women since his wife died, he would already have them behind bars. Don't worry, my boy can take care of himself." It was Granny adding her two cents worth.

Mary Ellen let Ira's Mother's comment go without acknowledgement. She had gotten used to the needling Granny enjoyed, never letting her forget that she knew the sheriff was one of her old boy friends.

It was almost too dark to recognize the passing automobiles; but when at last one came to a stop at the end of the lane, the family breathed a sigh of relief. The twins bailed off the porch and raced to open the gate.

"What did I tell you, all that worrying for nothing, I'm going to bed," Granny snorted.

Ira parked his squad car near the yard fence and pulled his tired frame from under the wheel. Mary Ellen greeted him with a firm hug and escorted him inside to the kitchen.

"What you need is a good hot meal."

"What I need is a different job! These young hot roding booze peddlers are going to be the death of me," he sighed.

"Don't say that Daddy," Mary Sue scolded as her parents disappeared inside.

The twins, feeling relieved that their father was home safely, went off to entertain themselves until bedtime.

Mary Sue and her older brother sat in silence for several moments. They were watching tiny fireflies light up their minute space in the vast darkening universe.

"What I need is a night on the town Little Sister, how about you?"

"Never had one," she smiled, "but it sure sounds like fun to me."

"Then put on your go-to-meeting clothes tomorrow night. You and I are going out and find ourselves a party."

CHAPTER TWO

THE STARLIGHT BALL ROOM

It was shortly after dusk when John Robert rounded the curve allowing the neon lights of the Starlight Ball Room to come into view. He eased his Chevy onto the crowded parking lot of the best-known entertainment establishment for many miles around. Several small groups of people were gathered near the front entrance as if waiting for something spectacular to take place. An occasional brown bag was being passed one to another, and each one seemed anxious to sample its contents.

Large funnel shaped loud speakers located on the edge of the roof near each corner of the long building were broadcasting the sounds of records being played on a jukebox inside.

Mary Sue started squirming in her seat as if she could not wait to bounce out of the car and rush inside. "What's everyone standing around outside for?" she wanted to know.

"They're waiting to be the first to greet the entertainer for tonight," her brother informed her.

"And who might that be?" she asked.

"Why, Hank Williams himself, I thought you knew."

"Hooray!" She screamed as she punched her big brother in the ribs. "You know I had no idea but thanks for letting it be a surprise."

Mary Sue settled back in her seat and with her arm resting on the open window began singing along with the voice from inside. It was Kitty Wells singing "Honky-Tonk Angels."

Her scream had been loud enough to attract the attention of a couple of young men who were standing nearby. The two fellows moved to either side of John Robert's car as if to introduce themselves.

"I'm Billy Joe Mayfield, but most folks call me Joe Boy," the fellow on her brother's side stated. "That young lady passenger of yours sure can sing," he added.

"No doubt about that," the young man who had approached Mary Sue's side agreed.

"My name is Eddie, Joe Boy's older brother; but you can tell by looking he must have been born a few years before me," he teased.

"My name is Mary Sue and this is my brother John Robert. You must also outrank him," she suggested, being aware of the corporal stripe on his service uniform. "How long have you been in the Army?"

"Twenty-one months, three more to go. Have you seen Hank before, in person I mean?"

"No and I can't wait," she answered unable to hide her excitement.

"Then you are about to," the young stranger stated as he opened the door allowing Mary Sue to step outside.

At that same moment a large blue Cadillac followed by a station wagon pulled into the parking space marked Reserved.

"It's Hank," someone yelled, and the small groups gathered on the parking began to converge on the vehicles that had just arrived.

Hank Williams exited the back seat of the Cadillac; and as Mary Sue caught sight of him, she almost fainted. He was dressed in blue jeans and a green plaid shirt but it was not hard to tell he was the real Hank Williams. Had it not been for the strong arm of the soldier she had just met she was sure she would have fallen to her knees.

Hank and his band were quickly escorted to another entrance toward the back of the building.

"He looks just like his picture on the cover of his latest album. Right, John Robert?"

"I was thinking more like Minnie Pearl," he joked. "Let's go inside while there is still room."

John Robert, his little sister, and the two young men they had just met squeezed through the main entrance just as the doorman sang out, "Sorry, All Sold Out."

As they stepped inside the dimly lit, smoke-filled room, Mary Sue became even more excited. Several rows of wooden folding chairs sat along either side of a large dance floor. One corner was hidden by a blue velvet curtain, which she assumed concealed the staging area. Multi-colored lights flickered as if keeping rhythm with the music being played on a jukebox. This was like nothing Mary Sue had ever seen but she knew at first glance she was going to enjoy the evening.

"Do you have a date for the night?" Eddie asked.

"Well, yeah - I mean not really,' she stammered.

"Then may I have this dance?" he asked as "The Tennessee Waltz" began playing on the jukebox.

Mary Sue looked at her brother for approval; and when he offered no objections she took the young soldier's hand and led him onto the dance floor. She had learned to dance in high school gym class and was among the best in her class. As the couple moved gracefully across the floor she discovered her partner had also mastered the art.

"Appears this is going to be another pleasant evening here at the Starlight," Eddie commented as the song ended.

"Sure does," she agreed, not wanting to admit that she had never been here or any other place similar to the Starlight in her life. "Do you come here often?"

"Not anymore, I've been away for almost two years."

Mary Sue was about to continue their conversation when all of a sudden the entire dance floor became brightly lit. A tall well-dressed gentleman stepped from behind the curtain onto the staging area and the crowd became silent. "It is now time to begin the live entertainment for the evening. Put your dancing shoes on, put your hands together and make welcome the one and only Mr. Hank Williams!"

It was at that moment the curtains slid open and the most popular entertainer of the decade stepped to center stage. The applause that followed was almost deafening. Unlike half-hour earlier he was now dressed in his usual western-style attire including his cowboy hat and boots. His first strum on his guitar brought his band to life.

"I Heard That Lonesome Whistle Blow" was Hanks introductory song and it brought the house down.

For the next hour he sang one hit after the other. The dance floor became more and more crowded and the applause became louder with the close of each tune. When it was time for intermission and the curtain closed, Mary Sue slumped into a chair near the stage.

"Would you care for something to drink?" Eddie asked.

"Yes, thanks; but no alcohol, please."

As Eddie crossed to the other side of the room to the concession corner she realized that she had danced with no one else the whole evening.

In a short while, he returned with two ice-cold bottles of Coca-Cola and sat in the seat beside her.

"You are a fantastic dance partner," he said.

"You're not so bad yourself," she started to say but was interrupted by a couple who came to where they were sitting.

"When did you get home, Eddie?" a pretty blonde lady wanted to know.

"Ten days ago."

"Why did you not let your old friends know you were back in town?" She spoke as if she had known Eddie for a long time.

"Just keeping a low profile I guess; I would like you to met Mary Sue," and then he began looking bewildered.

"Mary Sue Duncan," his dancing partner interrupted.

"I'm Judy Conley, and this fellow is my cousin Roy Lee," the lady continued as she reached to shake hands with Mary Sue. "I guess you know you have been dancing with the most eligible bachelor in these parts," she continued.

"I can see why; he is an excellent dancer," She could feel her face become flushed.

"I'm not much at dancing but I sure do like to listen to Old Hank sing," Roy Lee said as he also reached to shake hands with Mary Sue.

Mary Sue shook hands with the young stranger and determined that he must have just come from a logging job. His hands were as rough as sand paper and he had the grip of a grizzly bear.

A short time later the curtain opened for the second time and the band started playing. Judy grabbed Eddie by the hand and almost dragged him onto the dance floor. "I won't keep him long," she said to Mary Sue just before they disappeared among the other couples.

Mary Sue sat back in her chair that was directly in front of and facing the stage. She could not have been more than twenty feet from where Hank stood in front of a microphone. She began lip singing every song without missing a single word. After the third or fourth tune, Hank began to pay attention to what she was doing.

When at last Eddie was able to tear himself away from this Judy whatever-her-name-was and was about to ask Mary Sue for another dance, the song Hank was singing came to the end.

"I think I have an admirer who knows each of my songs by heart. I would be honored if she would come on stage and accompany me with the next number," Hank said as he extended a hand in Mary Sue's direction.

Shocked Mary Sue looked to either side to see whom he could be speaking about. "He can't mean me," she stammered, talking more to herself than anyone else

"I'm sure he does," Eddie said; and he took her by the hand and assisted her up on stage. Before she could hardly realize what was happening, she found herself standing side by side with one of the most famous country music singers of all time. To be in the same town where Hank Williams was performing was more than she could have ever dreamed. Now to be on stage with him was enough to make her the envy of every female in the in the county.

"What is your name?" Hank asked.

She looked out over the crowd and for the first time in her life she was almost speechless.

"Ma - Ma - Mary, Mary Sue Duncan," she was finally able to murmur.

"You must like country music," he continued.

"I sure do, sir," she spoke more clearly this time.

"What is your favorite song, and I do hope you pick one of mine," he teased.

"Anything you sing is one of my favorites," she admitted.

"Then let's sing," he shouted.

The band broke into one of his latest hits, "I'm So Lonesome I Could Cry", and to everyone's surprise Mary Sue joined in as if the two of them had rehearsed for hours. The duet sang until they came to the last verse. Then, Hank stepped back a few feet and directed Mary Sue to sing alone. She did so until they reached the chorus at which time Hank joined in. When the song ended the audience went wild. The only thing louder than the applause was Mary Sue's heartbeat.

"I think I may have just met the next female Grand Ole Opry Star, Miss Mary Sue Dunaway, give her another big hand," Hank said as his band burst into another of his latest hits.

Mary Sue's knees were so weak she could hardly get off stage even with Eddie's help. She was so excited she did not even mind that the Great Hank Williams had not remembered her last name. This was one evening she would remember for the remainder of her life.

"Can't leave you alone at all without you stealing the show; you were great, Sis." It was John Robert who was paying her the compliment this time.

"Where in the world did you learn to sing like that?" Eddie asked.

"Back on the farm. I've been practicing singing to the cows, pigs, and chickens, I guess," Mary Sue smiled.

"Then I guarantee your folks have the best milk, ham, and eggs in the county," he teased.

Mary Sue danced the next dance with her big brother. Her intentions had been to spend the remainder of the evening dancing with her newfound friend Eddie, but Miss Conley had other plans. Each time the couple took to the dance floor Conley would cut in. She pressed herself closer to Eddie than Mary Sue felt was lady-like and did not miss a chance to give her rival flaunting glances. As the evening wore on, Mary Sue had had enough of Conley's arrogance. Near the close of the show, she stood her ground. The next time Conley attempted to break in Mary Sue sharply remarked, "Not this time, Blondie; the rest of the night he belongs to me." Much sooner than she would have liked, the evening had come to an end and it was time to say goodbye.

"Will I see you again?" she asked as Eddie was walking her to where John Robert had parked his car.

"I sure hope so but it will be a while, I'll be leaving in the morning en route back to the base. I will be discharged in about three months, and I'll be looking for you here at the Starlight."

"If that's a promise, I'll be here every chance I get."

"It is," he smiled as he lightly kissed her forehead and turned to walk away.

Mary Sue watched as Conley grabbed his arm just before he disappeared into the shadows.

"That brazen blonde acts as if she has some sort of power over Eddie," she blurted as she slid into the passenger's seat and slammed the car door.

Her brother backed his Chevrolet onto the highway leaving the bright lights behind as they began the twenty-five mile trip back home.

"Well, what do you think of the wild side of life little sister?"

"I think it's great, I've never had so much fun. I can hardly wait for church in the morning so I can tell Pastor Kyle I got to sing with Hank Williams."

"I think I'd tell him I met Hank at an all day meeting. I don't think he'd appreciate knowing you spent tonight in a dance hall."

"I guess you're right," she snickered. "My feet are getting sore."

"Wonder why? You only danced three or four hours."

"You're right; Eddie was a great dancing partner."

"What is his last name, anyway?"

"Uh, I forget, Mayfield I think"

"Where is he from?"

"I forgot that, too, somewhere in the Carolinas."

"What do you know about him?"

"I know he is in the Army, he's good looking and a great dancer; and he thinks I can sing like a hummingbird. What else do I need to know, big brother?"

"That about covers it I guess,"

"Thanks for letting me tag along but you should have had a date yourself, John Robert."

The words were barely out of her mouth when she wished she could have taken them back. She knew quite well why he didn't have a date. He dated the prettiest girl in his class all through high school and was making plans to ask her to marry him soon after graduation. His plans were interrupted, however, when he received a letter from Uncle Sam informing him he was being drafted. His sweetheart had promised to wait for him but a short time after he left for service she married another man. Her brother never mentioned the young lady again, nor had he ever dated anyone else.

She was surprised she had not found out more about the soldier with whom she had spent the evening but it really didn't matter. She was determined not to get involved with anyone, as her sister had done, until she finished college. She fully intended to become a successful attorney; or maybe the next Grand Old Opry star Hank had mentioned.

She leaned back in her seat, slipped off her shoes, and rolled the window down letting the warm night airflow through her long black hair. She was grateful to her older brother for taking her someplace other than a movie theatre or a trip to their local skating rink. He was introducing her to greater adventures as he had done with Ida Mae.

She let her mind wander again to where her sister now lived and began daydreaming as the miles rolled by. She imagined all the things she and Ida Mae would do once she graduated and moved to North Carolina.

John Robert had accompanied her older sister to places she would not have been allowed to go alone. He had been the first to take Ida Mae inside a fancy restaurant, their hometown poolroom, and he had even taught her how to drive.

She let her mind wander again to where her sister now lived and began daydreaming as the miles rolled by. She imagined all things she and Ida Mae would do once she graduated and moved to North Carolina.

Before she realized how much time had passed, they stopped at the gate near the end of the lane leading to their home.

"I wish someone would invent an automatic opener," she complained as she exited the car to open the gate allowing her brother to pull through. She closed the gate behind him and jumped into the passenger's seat.

"When are you going to teach me how to drive like you did Ida Mae?" She asked.

"Now is as good a time as any I suppose. Get over here, little sister."

John Robert scooted to the passenger's side as Mary Sue ran barefooted around the front of the automobile and jumped into the driver's seat.

"Now put the car in gear, let out on the clutch, and give her some gas," he said.

Mary Sue did exactly as she was told, she put the Chevy in gear, let out on the clutch, and stomped the accelerator to the floor.

"Not that g . . . "

The car lurched backwards, went crashing through the gate, and came to rest with the rear bumper buried into the bank on the other side of the highway.

"Which gear did you mean?" She screamed.

John Robert got out of the car to determine the amount of damage his vehicle had suffered.

"Well looks like you have invented the automatic gate opener, Sis. What's your next project?"

"I'm so sorry John Robert, I'll help you fix it," she sobbed.

"Ah heck," he smiled. "Let's get home before we have an accident."

CHAPTER THREE

THE FAMILY GROWS SMALLER

Mary Sue crept quietly into the house with John Robert close behind. It was a few minutes past 2:00 a.m. and she'd never been out this late before. "I'll go on up to bed, " she whispered so as not to wake her parents whose bedroom was immediately to the left of the foot of the stairway.

"Think I'll see what's in the warming closet."

"You would," she giggled. "Good night."

"You young'uns have a good time?" came a voice out of the darkness.

Mary Sue was startled for a moment but not surprised that her mother would stay awake until she knew they were home safely.

"Sure did, Mom; tell you all about it in the morning," she answered as she bounded up the stairs taking two steps at a time.

She undressed and slipped between the cool freshly washed sheets. She was tired, her feet ached and she had to get up early for church, but she was far too excited to fall asleep.

She tried to figure how she would tell Preacher Kyle she had sung on stage with the Great Hank Williams without his knowing she had visited one of the areas most popular dance halls. After several explanations, none of which seemed believable, she decided to heck with Preacher Kyle; she would save her comments for Ida Mae.

She now had lots to tell her older sister, the excitement of her first visit to the liveliest nightspot for miles around, staying out later than she had ever done and dancing the night away with Eddie Maxfield – Moorefield – or whatever his last name was.

"Funny," she thought; she could not remember what her dancing partner's last name was or where he called home. Of little importance now, she decided. She was sure she could convince John Robert to take her back to the Starlight soon and she could find someone who knew the nice young soldier with whom she had enjoyed spending the evening, anyone except that rude Miss Conley! Had it not been for her many interruptions while she and Eddie were dancing, she would have found out more about him anyway. If she didn't, that would be all right. She most certainly wasn't going to let any handsome young fellow interfere with her plans to get a good education.

And, she needed to learn more about Jimmy Doug, Jake's brother, whom she had met a few days earlier. She felt it strange that he appeared so soon after the new sheriff was elected and was back in the mountains to help his family with some business ventures. Mary Sue knew quite well what his family's business had been in days gone by. The Hurd family was well known for being the best timber men in the logging business, but better known for making the best moonshine to ever pass the lips of those who enjoyed a toddy.

Mary Sue also began to share her mother's concern for her father's safety. Seemed he had to work longer hours, especially since the sheriff's wife had passed away. The tired look on her mother's face made it impossible to hide the concern she had for her spouse. Daddy was always home in time for the evening meal before the sheriff became a widower. But since then, her mother had been spending much more time after supper waiting for his return. Maybe Granny was right; Baxter might be spending much more time chasing women than he was trying to put a stop to the flow of shine through the county. She, on the other hand, put little stock in Granny's comments about the sheriff. The comments readily implied Baxter still had eyes for her mother.

She wished her daddy could find better employment; but since it was so soon after the end of the war and many jobs were being taken by returning soldiers, jobs were hard to find. After all, her father had done little in his life except sharecrop and he was not qualified for skilled labor.

No time to think of these things now. She fluffed her pillow, turned on her side to watch the shadows created by the floating clouds as they passed in front of the bright shining moon. Eddie Mayfield, that was the young soldier's name, she remembered; and he was really quite handsome she had to admit. These were her last thoughts as she was overtaken by a peaceful slumber.

* * * * * *

"Rise and shine," It was Granny's shrill voice calling from half way down the staircase. "Just because you see fit to stay out all night and half the morning doesn't mean you get to stay in bed and sleep all day. It is Sunday morning and we have to go to church you know."

Mary Sue could hardly believe it was already time to get out of bed. She had awakened only moments earlier while in the middle of a wonderful dream about singing on stage at the Grand Ole Opry. Now that she was trying to go back to sleep and resume her fantasy dream, Granny found cause to spoil it.

She sat up on the side of her bed while trying to put together the happenings of the night before. She likened them to the times when her older sister Ida Mae came home excited about a night out. She wished Ida Mae were here now so she would have someone with whom she could share her innermost feelings. Slipping into one of her Sunday dresses she rushed down stairs to start the day.

The smell of fresh brewed coffee and country bacon frying filled the crisp morning air. Being Sunday, she knew her mother was preparing the best breakfast of the week. It was the only day

Daddy did not have to work and the whole family could enjoy their morning meal together. They would then be off to morning worship service to listen to Preacher Kyle remind everyone about how to live if they expected to get to Heaven. That is everyone except Granny. She always sat at the end of the pew close to the wall and was most always asleep before the end of the second hymn. When anyone made a comment about her behavior, she would reply, "At my age I could do little that would be sinning anyway."

As usual the Duncan family was up on Sunday morning at least a couple of hours before church time. They used this time to reflect on the happenings of the previous week and make plans for the upcoming days ahead. Today was no different from any other Sunday morning. The whole family was seated waiting for Granny to take her place next to her son at the head of the table. She seemed to make it a point to be the last to arrive so everyone would have to wait for her before they begin eating, a simple reminder that she deserved and expected their respect.

Just before Kevin, one of the twins, started to make some off the wall comment about her being late again, Granny found her place and sat down. She removed the upper portion of her false teeth from her apron pocket, blew off any dust particles they might have collected and placed them in her mouth.

"Pass the gravy, Ira," she stammered. "Think that's about all I can handle this morning. Too many interruptions to get any rest, what with all the noise these young folks make coming home so late."

"Then why do you have to have them store-bought teeth if you ain't going to eat nothing but gravy?" Kervin, the other twin, wanted to know.

"Did you two have a good time?" Ira questioned.

"Wonderful," Mary Sue blurted. "I met the most exciting young soldier and we danced most of the night away."

"Well, what do you know, big sister done got her a feller?" Kevin snickered.

"I also sang on stage with Mr. Hank Williams, smarty pants," Mary Sue continued unable to hide her enthusiasm to share her experience with the entire family.

"Yeah, and I took my Saturday night bath with the Pope," Kervin said laughing more loudly this time.

"She'll be married and gone off like Ida Mae in a couple of months I suppose," Kevin agreed.

"That's enough boys," their mother scolded. "Finish your breakfast and go play until time for service."

The twins did as they were told, and the morning ended with little other to-do.

"I would like to talk to you about a matter that's been on my mind for some time, Daddy," John Robert spoke as the ladies began to clear the dishes.

"Sure enough," Ira replied, as he arose and led the way to the front porch. He was well aware that something was bothering his oldest son, but he also knew that John Robert would discuss it at a time of his own choosing. With John Robert's work every weekday in the fields and spending his weekends in town, Ira had seen very little of his son for the past few weeks. Especially since most of his own time was taken up by duties assigned to him by the sheriff.

The two men seated themselves side-by-side atop the wide steps that led from the front porch of their two-story farmhouse to the front yard. Several moments passed before either of them spoke.

"It's been a good year, Daddy," John Robert said as they stared down over the large fields of corn ready to be harvested and the huge stacks of hay ready to be fed to the sheriff's increasing herd of cattle.

"Best ever," his daddy answered. "Now that you have taken over running the farm and me having the job as chief deputy, the Duncan family's lifestyle has drastically improved, if I do say so myself. Your sister has started a new life in the Carolinas with the man of her dreams and enough money to begin raising a family if they chose. Mary Sue will be finishing her senior year in a few months; the twins need nothing I am aware of and even Granny finds less to complain about lately. Reckon we could say it's been a good year," Ira concluded.

"Which brings me to what I wanted to talk to you about," John Robert began. "Me and some of the guys in town have decided to go to the other end of the state to find a job. Since the end of the war, the shipyards out on the coast are hiring folks as fast as they can put them on the payroll. They are paying top wages and ex-service personnel have priority. I wouldn't leave until all the crops are in, of course," he continued. "The sheriff is making enough money to hire the farm work done come spring; and with our family growing smaller you and Mom can take life easier without working so hard—once your feller's rid the county of those moonshine runners," he added.

This came as no surprise to Ira. He had little expected John Robert to return to the farm after his tour in the army. Knowing his son's interest in automobile engines and his ability to make them run faster, he anticipated he would some day seek a position with a car manufacturer.

"Only you know what's best," Ira said. "It's sure going to be hard on your mother and me to see you leave home again. When you plan on leaving?"

"Sometime soon after Christmas, I suppose. I better go up and get dressed or the family will be going to church without me."

CHAPTER FOUR

EARLY AUTUMN

Summer on the Baxter farm flew by. Most of the farm crops were harvested. Mary Ellen, Granny, with help from the twins were busying themselves storing and preserving food for the winter. Mary Sue was settling into her senior year, working hard to be among the best in her class. She and Ida Mae were writing each other at least twice a week. It was difficult to tell which was more excited about the two of them being together in Winston Salem.

The only thing that did not seem to be going well for the Duncan family was the progress with the whiskey runners. Ira was continuing to come home later day after day, many times so tired he could barely stay awake long enough to eat his supper. And, to make matters worse, the sheriff was becoming more critical of his deputy's accomplishments although he did little to aid in the cause himself. The rumor had it that Baxter was doing quite a bit of running, but it was in pursuit of the opposite sex rather than the bootleggers.

Mary Sue was concerned about the well being of her daddy. She felt that, in time, the matter of illegal whiskey running would come to a head and the guilty parties would be behind bars. She tried not to let matters outside her schoolwork occupy her mind.

The school assignment was her next task for this beautiful afternoon, but first she was going to make her daily trip to the mailbox. She walked the few hundred few down the lane leading to the graveled road. She had not heard from Ida Mae since she had written about the good-looking soldier she met at the ballroom. Just as she was about to open the mailbox a familiar looking vehicle came to a stop near where she was standing.

"Hello, Pretty Lady, are you expecting a love letter?" someone asked.

"Why, hello, fellows." Mary Sue recognized J.D. and her brother-in-law Jake, and the vehicle was the one she remembered seeing earlier in the summer.

"As a matter fact, I'm expecting a letter from my big sister," she smiled.

Jake extracted an envelope from over the sun visor and handed it to Mary Sue. "Special delivery," he said.

She slipped the letter into the pocket of her dress. She would have to read it later. "What are you boys doing in this part of the country, after a load of that good shine?" she inquired, remembering the comment J.D. had made during their only other meeting.

"Delivered it last week," Jake's brother teased. "We just stopped by to say hello.

We're headed across the mountain to visit out parents. Daddy's health has not been good as of late, and we decided to come home for a day or two. Thought we might find some of the good old boys we grew up with to give him a hand with the logging business until he gets back on his feet."

"Jump in," Jake said, "no use you walking back up to the house." He leaned the back of the passenger seat forward allowing Mary Sue room to climb into the back.

"Smells brand spanking new," she commented, as she sank into the leather upholstery.

"Sure is," J.D. was quick to answer. Just bought her two days before I came by here back in the summer. I was on my way to

Winston that very day to have some of those hot rod mechanics rebuild the engine. They sure did a fine job too, oversized pistons, dual carburetors, straight pipes, the works. She'll outrun almost anything on the road, right Jake?"

Before Jake could answer Mary Sue asked, "Why in the world would you want to do all that to a brand new automobile?"

"Racing sweetheart, racing is becoming big business, especially in the Carolinas.

Some of them old boys are willing to bet their entire paycheck on who has the fastest machine. Now that I got the Green Dragon souped up, I plan to spend some of their money. Come on down and visit Jake and Ida Mae some weekend and watch us go at it."

"Funny name for a car," she said. "Is it really that fast?"

"Hang on," J.D. answered as he shifted the big green machine into gear. He stomped the accelerator to the floor and Mary Sue felt as if her back was being pressed against the seat. The sound of the roaring engine reminded her of one of the low flying jets that sometimes flew over. She could hear gravels flying from beneath the rear wheels; and before she had time for another thought, they were stopped in front of the yard gate.

"What were you asking?" J.D. questioned.

"Nothing, I guess," she squeaked, as she sucked in a long breath. "You boys come on in; Mother should have supper ready and Daddy should be home at any time."

"Sounds good to me," Jake replied. "I haven't had one of your mom's delicious meals in a long time, and Ida Mae is constantly making comments about what a wonderful cook she is."

The brothers followed Mary Sue onto the porch where the twins were waiting with at least a hundred questions.

"You fellows make yourself at home while I go inside and tell Mother and Granny we have company."

She was barely out of sight when Kevin's questions started coming.

"How fast will that car run? Why did you pick that ugly green? How much did it cost?" Kevin was firing the questions at J.D. faster than he could answer.

"About a hundred and twenty, so I could hide her in the trees, and more than I like to think about," J.D. answered when the young fellow slowed down long enough for him to get a word in. Everything he said was true, but he wished he had left out the part about being able to hide his car in the trees.

Kervin showed little interest in their conversation about the automobile. He was questioning Jake, who was seated on the opposite end of the porch, about other matters. "Been shooting pool lately? Been winning any money like you did when Dooley was still around?"

"Very little pool shooting going on now, Kervin; your big sister keeps me busy. I haven't won any money lately either; guess I'm getting a little rusty."

Mary Sue reappeared just before the next barrage of questioning began. Granny followed close behind and next came Mary Ellen carrying a large cool glass of apple cider for each of their guests.

J.D. was first to sample the refreshing liquid. "Thanks ma'am, this is almost as good as the apple brandy Daddy mak . . . " he hesitated, "used to make."

Mary Ellen sat beside Jake in the porch swing and began asking him about Ida Mae and life in the big city. Granny pulled a straight-backed chair as close as possible so she wouldn't miss any of the conversation. After all, tomorrow was the next meeting of her ladies' group, and she was not about to miss out on any good gossip. There sure had not been much going on with the sheriff's department to talk about lately.

John Robert soon joined the group and the conversation once again returned to J.D's new set of wheels. The ladies, all except Granny, excused themselves to finish preparing the evening meal.

The young men talked about everything: hunting, fishing, farming, police work, fast cars, and politics. J. D. pretended to be interested in all they talked about; but at every opportunity, he inquired about the illegal whiskey traffic through the county.

"Daddy doesn't talk much about that," John Robert informed him. "I guess he doesn't want to worry Mother." He continued with small talk about other topics until he caught Granny's head turned. The moment she looked in another direction he signaled the Hurd brothers to follow him, indicating he needed to speak to them in private. "Sure would like to see what's under the hood of that flying machine you fellers are driving. Would you mind if we take a look while we're waiting for supper?"

Both Jake and J.D. got the message. As the threesome made their way to where the new automobile was parked, Granny made her way to the bottom step. John Robert was sure she was out of hearing distance but he lowered his voice as a precautionary measure. J.D. raised the hood of the Dodge, and John Robert pretended to be interested in all the chrome that came into view.

"I've been really concerned about Daddy," John Robert told them. "The sheriff is constantly putting pressure on all his deputies to step up their efforts to catch those fellers running moonshine. I don't think he is as interested in catching them as he is in making himself look like a hero, but it's not the actual chasing I'm concerned about. Some of Fletcher's old cronies have been making threats about getting even with those who caused his death. Every day Daddy comes home late, I get more concerned that some of those threats might be carried out. I found a note under one of the windshield wipers of his cruiser the other morning informing him to tell Baxter to back off. I never mentioned this to Mother, you understand, she has enough fearful thoughts of her own."

"Have any thoughts about who's making the threats?" Jake asked.

"No, but they are becoming more serious. Fletcher did have some old friends who would take more pleasure in getting revenge than selling their shine. I have someone trying to find out about the threats but nothing has turned up so far."

33

"Someone whom you can really trust, I hope."

"Sure enough, he's a cop himself."

"Someone I know?"

J.D. leaned a little closer so he could hear more clearly.

"Oh, yeah, it . . . "

"Come and get it," Mary Sue called from the front door. The invitation only had to be given once.

"Sure is a fast moving machine, J.D. I'm sure glad you're into auto racing instead of moonshine running," John Robert commented as he led the brothers into the kitchen.

The conversation at the supper table bounced from subject to subject but for the most part centered around Ira and his work. He was expected to arrive at any moment but that didn't happen. After the meal was finished Mary Sue suggested that everyone find someplace more comfortable while she cleaned the dishes.

"May I help," J.D. offered, "to show my appreciation for such a fine supper?"

Mary Sue was about to decline his offer when Granny interrupted. "Sure, you can take my place. I'm especially tired today; and if you don't mind, I'll just go sit with the others."

"Still seeking information to share at tomorrow's hen party," Mary Sue thought but she offered no further objections. "I'll wash and you can dry," she told her guest. For several moments there was only silence. At last Mary Sue asked, "What type of work do you do J.D.?"

"Nothing at this time."

"You mean you don't have a job? How on earth are you able to make payments on such a fine automobile?"

"Don't have any payments," he lied

Mary Sue was so surprised she almost dropped the plate she had just finished washing. "Sorry, I really didn't mean to pry."

J.D. smiled at her bewilderment. "That's all right. I worked in a GM plant up north for almost five years so I got a really good deal. I would still be there except I got laid off this summer. The company offered special pricing to those of us who were losing their jobs, and I took it. I had saved enough money to pay cash."

"What are you planning to do now? Uh Oh, prying again."

"I'm not really sure. Jake and I are going to spend a few days with Mom and Dad and then go back to Winston Salem for a while I suppose."

"Going to find a job in Winston?"

"Not for a while. I still have a few bucks left so I think I will hang out with my big brother. It been a while since we've spent much time together, might even take him and Ida Mae out to some nightspots to hear some good music."

"What kind of music?"

"Country, is there any other kind?"

"Not as far as I'm concerned. I love country music. Is there a lot of country music bands in Winston?"

"All over the place. Some of the most famous country entertainers of today got their start in some of the biggest nightclubs in and around Winston. Some of the best musicians, too I might add."

"Have you ever seen Hank Williams?"

"Several times, he's my favorite. As a matter of fact I believe he's everyone's favorite."

This made Mary Sue even more excited about her upcoming move to the big city. She was about to delve into more conversation about their mutual love for county music when Jake appeared in the doorway. "Time to hit the road if we are going to get to the other side of the mountain before dark."

J.D. agreed. He folded the dishtowel, placed it gently on one of Mary Sue's shoulders and thanked her again for the wonderful meal.

She followed the two young men to the very edge of the front porch. "You'll come back again, won't you? I just have to learn more about those nightclubs."

"I hope to be around quite often," he assured her. "I'll stop every chance I get."

The brothers were about to get into the Dodge as Ira's police car stopped at the end of the lane. It was getting late but Jake was not about to leave without at least saying hello to his father-in-law.

Ira pulled his cruiser along side the Dodge. "Hey there, Jake," he smiled, "you fellows are sure riding in style."

"Just a passenger," Jake volunteered. "This is my brother Jimmy Doug, these wheels belong to him."

J.D. extended his hand. "Pleased to meet you Officer Duncan. How have you been?"

"Been wasting my time chasing young fellers like you two driving new cars for the most part, and just call me Ira."

"Finding any white liquor?"

"Not much but I am writing a passel of speeding tickets."

Jake could see Ira looked extremely tired. "Why aren't you fellows having any luck?"

"Those boys are smart, they are using those hotrods as decoys while moving the moonshine by some other means. Deputy Barton and I have decided we won't try to stop anything that even looks new."

"You mean Howard Barton? Is he still around?" Jake asked.

"You bet. Howard and I try to chase the whiskey runners while the boss chases women; and from what I hear, he's having far more success than we are."

"Better get going, Jake, if we don't get started soon Mom and Dad will be in bed before we get there."

"See you in a few days Ira," Jake told him as he jumped into the front seat and his brother started the engine.

Ira waved as they were leaving. "You boys take it easy through the rest of the county. Howard's out there somewhere and that machine might make him change his mind about stopping anything that looks new."

J.D. was careful not to sound off those straight pipes that replaced the mufflers or send gravels flying as he had done upon their arrival.

Mary Sue followed her parents into the kitchen. She watched as her mother filled her daddy's plate from containers of food still being kept warm on top of their wood-burning cook stove. She placed small portions onto another plate and seated herself near him. It didn't matter that she had eaten a few bites with the others she always had her evening meal with her husband.

Mary Sue was grateful for the admiration her parents had for each other. She could not help but notice the aging lines being formed on each of their faces. Although financially life was better now than she could ever remember, she wondered if the stress they were under was worth it. She needed to go to her room to finish her assignments for the following day but she stood for a moment watching as her mother moved a little closer to her father. This was quality time for them and she did not choose to interrupt. It was these moments she was sure she would recall years after her life on the farm was past. Ida Mae made mention of such moments many times in her letters.

Her letter! Suddenly she remembered the letter. Mary Sue climbed the stairs to her room, stretched herself on her bed and opened the envelope. As usual she was anxious to hear about what was going on with her older sister. Ida Mae never failed to have something new and exciting to share with her. Sometimes it was a sporting event, a new place to dine, shop or the latest movie she had seen. Occasionally she would tell something about attending a live performance by a country music entertainer. This was the subject that most interested Mary Sue. And, it was what made her more anxious for graduation. After that she would be able to do all the things her sister wrote about. If she were lucky, she might even get to see Hank Williams again.

Ida Mae told her about new guests visiting their home and about J.D.'s visit to Winston. She told how he and Jake were planning to spend time up in the mountains helping their daddy rebuild his logging business. She did not like the idea of Jake being away most of the winter but at last agreed he could go if he promised to be home at least every other weekend.

Mary Sue was beaming with excitement as she folded the letter. She placed it in the top drawer of her dresser along with all the others. Ida Mae was not only her sister; she was her best friend. She sat on a small bench in front of her window and recalled the many times they had sat here together and talked secretly about their dreams of the future. Things had turned out much differently than her sister had hoped, but at last, she was happy.

Chapter Five

BACK TO THE BALLROOM

Fall in the mountains of Virginia was a busy time of the year. Farmers rushed to get their crops harvested before the bitter chill of winter. The women folks busied themselves storing food for their family, and the young ones began looking to the coming of Christmas. It was also the time when Mother Nature adorned her garments with unmatched beauty. Early morning dewdrops glistened like diamonds clinging to multi-colored leaves. Warm morning breezes dried them, and the autumn sunrays set them ablaze.

Mary Sue and Granny sat on the porch talking of days gone by. It was not often they spent time together alone. They sat for some time in silence, each seeming to be consumed by some far-away thoughts. Mary Ellen was adding the last touches to their evening meal; the twins were out near the barn helping John Robert adjust the brakes on his Chevy and Ira was still at work.

"He's getting ready to leave us for good this time, I guess," Granny said.

"Who?"

"John Robert. He's getting his car all tuned up for the trip out to the other end of the state. I heard him tell his mother he was leaving right after the Christmas holiday. Looks like all the young'uns will be gone before me," she whimpered.

"Where you going?" The words had barely escaped her lips until Mary Sue was sorry she had asked.

"Off to the poor farm probably."

"Thought you were still looking for some handsome rich fellow to come along and carry you off," Mary Sue teased.

"Sorta give up on that when Brother Taylor passed on," she admitted. "Never figured out why he didn't want to sit beside me in church."

"Maybe he didn't want to hear you snore," Mary Sue thought but felt it better to keep this thought to herself.

"First, it was your sister; now, it's John Robert; and you will be leaving in the spring," Granny continued. "I guess the twins will be around for a few more years and then they will be off somewhere, too. That would just leave me here with your mommy while Ira is off chasing bootleggers. Ain't likely our woman-chasing sheriff is going to have any of them rounded up any time soon." She leaned forward in her rocker and stared through the screen door to assure herself that no one else could hear. "Never have liked him since he was caught cheating on your mother. That was a few days before she and your daddy were married," she quickly added.

Mary Sue knew all too well that her mother and the sheriff had dated for a short time before she and her father married. She also knew that Granny had suspicions as to whether John Robert was really her grandson, although that suspicion was never voiced when her daddy was present.

Mary Sue chose to ignore Granny's last statement. She left her alone on the porch and went to where her brothers were working. "How are you coming along, fellows?"

"Got her purring like a kitten," Kervin volunteered as if he had done most of the work.

John Robert closed the hood of his Chevy and sat on the front bumper. Mary Sue sat down beside him and the twins went off to check on supper.

"In a few weeks you will be leaving," she reminded him.

"I know, but I'll be home real often; it won't be like when I was in service."

"Yes, but I won't be here. I'll be in North Carolina."

"So! That's not exactly the end of the world. I think I can find my way to Winston to see you girls."

"Thanks for teaching me to drive, taking me to the ballroom and all the other wonderful things you have done for me since you've been out of the army. John Robert, I'm sure going to miss you."

"That reminds me, do you have any plans for Saturday night? If you don't, I thought we might go back to the Starlight." The words were barely out of his mouth when their mother called from the porch, "Supper's ready."

Mary Sue leaped from the bumper, threw her hands in the air, and yelled "THAT'S GREAT! If I did have, they just got cancelled!"

"She must really be starved," Granny grunted as she followed Mary Ellen back into the house.

Mary Sue could hardly wait to get up to her room to get a letter off to her sister. Since the beginning of her senior year she had done little else but study. She was sure her letters to Ida Mae were sometimes boring, but now she now had something really exciting to share with her. Her grades were excellent; the Thanksgiving holiday plans were falling into place, and she was going back to the Starlight Ball Room.

She was so excited she had failed to ask her brother who was going to be the featured entertainer, but it didn't really matter. She knew she was going to have a wonderful evening. "I might even get to dance with Eddie again," she wrote. She finished the longest letter she had ever written and closed with "I love you and I can hardly wait for us to share more good times together."

She hoped Ida Mae would be able to share a bit of her excitement. She was aware that her sister was really depressed. Jake's role in getting his daddy's business off the ground was getting to be more and more time consuming, and he was coming home far less often. J.D., on the other hand, was back in Winston practically every weekend. He had his eyes on some good-looking lady at one of the bars just outside of town, at least that was what he was telling his family. He seldom stopped by Chestnut Street and that suited Ida Mae just fine. Because of Jake she held her temper, but she was becoming more annoyed with J.D. each passing day. She felt he was not sharing his part of the responsibility of rebuilding his father's business and that was keeping Jake away from home.

"One day I will really give J.D. a piece of my mind," she told Mary Sue in one of her letters.

The week following John Robert's invitation to take Mary Sue back to the ballroom was the happiest time of her senior year. She was the envy of every girl in her class for having been on stage with Hank Williams. She was not about to fail to give them the opportunity to wonder whom she might meet next.

The week passed quickly; and before she knew it, she was getting dressed for her second big night out. When she finished, she stood before her full-length mirror to make sure everything looked just as she wanted. It was only then she realized she was wearing the same blue dress Ida Mae had worn the first time she went out with Dooley. She went down the stairs and stepped into the late afternoon sunlight. Her family had never seen her look more beautiful.

"Well, now, don't you look just stunning? I'll have to keep my eyes on you tonight," John Robert assured her.

"Not bad for a country bumpkin," Kervin teased.

"She is a good-looking pumpkin," Kevin giggled as he added his two cents worth.

"I'll settle with you two when I'm not all dressed up," she promised.

Mary Sue hugged her mother tightly and whispered, "Thanks, Mom, I'll always make you proud of me." She turned and started to walk away just as her mother dabbed a tear forming in the corner of her eye. She knew her mother was saddened at seeing the last of her two girls rapidly becoming a woman.

"That girl will be married before the next corn cutting," Granny said more to herself than anyone else.

John Robert took her by the hand and led her to the driver's side of his Chevy. He opened the door and motioned for her to be seated.

"Am I driving?"

"Only if we take the back way; could be a lawman out there, you know."

Mary Sue started the Chevy and shifted into gear. She waved and moved the car forward as if she had years of experience behind the wheel. She drove the entire distance to the dance hall without making a single mistake.

"Might as well take you to make your license before I leave for the coast, young lady; you did great."

John Robert escorted her into the crowded building and led her to the concession area. He purchased a cold soft drink for each of them and found a seat near the corner of the stage. In a short while, a local band started playing. She listened to the music, which wasn't at all bad, and watched as couples began crowding onto the floor. Before the second tune ended a young gentleman was asking her for her first dance. He was by far not the most handsome fellow there, but she accepted his offer. This way she could scan the dance floor for anyone she knew, anyone by the name of Eddie. It was almost impossible to see anyone while sitting down.

She waltzed with several fellows while searching the dance floor for the soldier she had met during her last visit. By the time the evening was half gone she convinced herself he was not going to show. It was during one of the waltz numbers that Roy Lee, Judy Conley's cousin, asked her partner if he might break in. He was the fellow she remembered with the rough skin-cracked hands, and the one she was soon to learn had two left feet.

"How have you been?" he asked. "Haven't seen you around since the night you sang with Ole Hank."

She turned her face away so as not to be knocked off her feet by his alcohol-laden breath. Before he could say anything else she asked, "Where's Eddie?"

"Off somewhere playing I reckon," he slurred. Before she could ask what he meant the dance ended. "Ask Judy, she's over yonder with some of her buddies," he mumbled as he staggered away. (She later learned he was escorted away from the premises and given free lodging in the local jail for the night.)

She danced to a few more tunes; and as the night was coming to a close, she decided that if she were to learn anything about the young soldier she would have to approach the blonde whom she disliked. As difficult as it was, she made her way to where Judy was entertaining three or four men with some off-colored jokes. "Hello," she said, "How come I haven't seen you with your boy-friend tonight?"

"Which one?" she giggled.

"Why Eddie," she said, embarrassed," the handsome young soldier I met here a few weeks ago."

"He's not my boyfriend, least ways not anymore. Ain't you the gal that sang with Hank Williams?"

"Sure am." she said proudly.

"You're pretty good, sweetie; matter of a fact, you're real good. You and Eddie should get together, seeing as how you both like to sing; and he is the best guitar picker for miles around."

"What ever happened to him?" Mary Sue asked, feeling her-self blush.

"The way I heard it he traded his uniform for a guitar and headed south to play with a well-known band."

Mary Sue thanked her and turned to walk away.

"Might as well to give up on Eddie. Ain't nobody going to tie that feller down; believe me, I tried."

Mary Sue did not reply; instead, she headed for the exit where she knew John Robert would be waiting.

"Ready to go home?" he asked.

"May I drive?"

"You bet." He knew he would be leaving home in a few weeks and he wanted this outing with his little sister to be as memorable as he could make it.

"Have a good time?" he asked.

"It was nice but I didn't get to see . . . " she hesitated.

"The young soldier."

"The young soldier," she smiled.

"What do you think about Jake being here in the mountains so much?" she asked, wanting to change the subject. "Ida Mae is concerned because he spends too much time away from home, and J.D. spends too much time away from the job."

"Something's not right," he agreed, "but I'm sure they'll work it out."

"Why do families have to become so scattered, John Robert?"

Detecting a bit of sadness in her voice he replied, "Different interest, I guess. We'll just have to start having a family reunion."

"That's a great idea. Jake promised to bring Ida Mae home next week so we could all be together. We'll have our first family reunion on Thanksgiving."

It was almost midnight by the time they got back home. Just as they were about to stop at the end of the lane they saw their daddy's police car approaching from the opposite direction.

John Robert opened the gate and both vehicles pulled through. Mary Sue was surprised when the red lights atop the patrol car started flashing. Before she knew what was happening Ira was standing beside the Chevy with ticket book in hand. He shined his flashlight inside as he spoke. "May I see your driver's license, please?"

"I don't have one, sir," she said pretending to be really frightened. "I hope you are not going to write me up."

Her daddy stepped to the rear of the car, wrote something in the ticket book, came back to the driver's side and handed her what appeared to be a legal sheet of paper. Again he shined his flashlight inside the Chevy. She smiled as she read, "You sure look beautiful tonight, and I'm so proud of you."

"I'm proud of you, too, Daddy," she smiled.

Ira followed the couple to where they parked in front of the yard gate. As they got out of their vehicles, he heard John Robert say to his little sister, "That cop must have been in a good mood tonight or he would have given you a ticket."

"I am." Ira said, "Just locked up two fellows from over in the next county. They were so drunk they probably won't know where they are until they sober up in the morning. They won't know what happened to the five gallon of shine they were hauling either until I let them know it's locked up in the evidence room."

"That's why you are out so late; I bet the sheriff is pleased."

"Shucks, he doesn't know what's going on. No one has seen him for two or three days."

The very next day Mary Sue started making plans for the Thanksgiving Day festivities. Immediately after church she and her mother made a list of items needed from the grocery store in town. John Robert would make sure to get everything the following day. The twins were given instructions on how to make wreaths of leaves and wild grape vines. Granny volunteered to make her mouth-watering dressing, a secret recipe she shared with no one.

The holiday was only four days away and school was out for the entire week. Mary Sue had ample time to help prepare the turkey and all the trimmings. The Duncan family was going to be together for the first time since Ida Mae had left home. She was determined to make this a reunion to remember.

Chapter Six

THE FIRST REUNION

The day before Thanksgiving was an unusually warm day for late November and everyone in the Duncan family was getting more and more excited about the upcoming festivities. Granny and Mary Ellen were in the kitchen double-checking the menu for the next day's meal. Ira, who was taking a few days off from his police duties, John Robert and the twins were all enjoying a game of horseshoe out near the tool shed. Mary Sue sat at her favorite daydreaming getaway near the springhouse. She leaned against the willow tree, dangled her feet in the spring's cool overflow and let her face soak in the warmth of the setting autumn sun. Like everyone else, she anxiously awaited the arrival of Jake and Ida Mae; and from where she sat, she would be the first one to see them come into view.

She was happy that Ida Mae was coming back home to spend a few days, and that the family would all be together for the first time in months. But, she was also saddened at the thought of what the days that lay ahead would bring. Before the beginning of spring, life on the Baxter was sure to change. Ida Mae would be back in the Carolinas, John Robert in the far end of the state; and she, too, would be making plans to leave home.

She was about to allow herself to become more melancholy with the thought of leaving the family when she was startled by the loud sound of an automobile horn. It was Jake making everyone aware of Ida Mae's arrival. She didn't even take time to put on her slippers. She grabbed one with each hand and ran barefoot through the tall grass toward the farm entrance gate. She slung the gate open for Jake to pull through without coming to a stop. Ida Mae was out of the car and the sisters were wrapped in a tight embrace almost before it stopped moving.

"We'll walk," Ida Mae told Jake as she motioned for him to drive on. "You're still a country girl I see," she smiled as she pointed to her sister's bare feet.

"Yep."

"Me too."

She hurriedly removed her own shoes, reached for Mary Sue's and tossed both pair into the back seat. The girls held hands and began walking up the lane as they had done a hundred times before.

"How long will you be home, Sis?" Mary Sue wanted to know.

"Until Sunday evening."

"That's almost four days; we have a million things to talk about. Think maybe we can cover half of them?"

"Not in four days," Ida Mae assured her. The sisters tightened their clasped hands and went running up the lane.

Jake visited for a while and then excused himself to go have Thanksgiving dinner with his parents, but he promised to be back the following day before all the leftovers were gone. These arrangements were fine with Ida Mae, and she sent word that she would come visit before going back to Winston.

The next four days was filled with fun and excitement. Life on the farm was once more as it had been before any of the children left home.

Every member of the Duncan family was up before sunrise Thanksgiving morning. There was a slight chill in the air and light frost was beginning to appear as the darkness of night gave way to dawn.

Ida Mae was the first one of the girls to start down stairs. The aroma of freshly brewed coffee and country-fried ham filled her nostrils before she was halfway to the bottom. She hesitated for a moment, savoring the fond memories of days gone by. From where she stood, she could see her daddy and three brothers encircling the warm morning wood burner that furnished the only heat source for the front portion of their home.

Her daddy was cleaning one of his twelve-gauge shotguns that would be used in the rabbit hunt following breakfast. Until John Robert's leaving for the army, a rabbit hunt on Thanksgiving morning was a long-standing Duncan family tradition. The twins were never before allowed to carry guns but they were permitted to tag along if they chose. Today, however, they were going to take turns firing their daddy's twenty-two rifle, if they were lucky enough to find a rabbit to shoot.

The twins were questioning their father as to how he had managed to catch the two fellers he'd locked up the night before. She was sure they were preparing themselves for some dramatic story about a high-speed chase that ended in a capture that would make him look like a hero. They seemed disappointed when he told them Officer Barton informed him they would be traveling through the county and would most likely be carrying a few jugs of whiskey. All he had to do was watch for their arrival and pull them over. The arrest took place without incident.

"Did they rat on whoever was making the booze?" One of the twins asked.

"Too intoxicated for any sensible information, but one of them did mumble something about having a friend from Chicago who would have them out of jail before daylight."

Mary Sue came downstairs a short time later. She walked past the doorway on her way to the kitchen just as the twins began arguing about which one was to be the first to carry the rifle.

John Robert was also cleaning the gun he would be using and seemed to be paying little attention to what was being said until his daddy made the comment about the fellow from Chicago. Suddenly, he remembered Mary Sue telling him that was where

Jake's brother hailed from. He opened his mouth and was almost ready to speak as the breakfast call came from the kitchen. Hunger pains sent his daddy and his two little brothers hurrying to answer the call. "Just as well," he thought. The Hurd family suffered too great a loss when Fletcher was sheriff to ever get involved in making moonshine again. He dismissed the thought and followed the other guys into the kitchen.

The last one to the table was Mary Sue. She came rushing into the kitchen apologizing for being late and whispered something into her daddy's ear before taking her place beside Ida Mae.

As soon as she was seated, Ira asked everyone to bow his head. He asked the Lord to bless their food and thanked Him for allowing all his family members to be present at his table. Immediately following Amen, he added, "Mary Sue wants each of us to promise we will always come back home for our reunion on Thanksgiving."

"And hurry up," Kervin insisted, "I'm starved."

One by one they each agreed to her request.

The twins gobbled down their food while continuing their dispute about the rifle. At last it was Granny who offered a solution. She removed a silver dollar from the pocket of her apron and suggested they flip for the honor.

"Suits me," Kervin said.

"Me, too," Kevin snapped, "I want heads."

"That's what I wanted," Kervin answered. It was evident another argument was about to take place.

"Tell you what," Granny interrupted. "Kevin gets heads, Kervin gets tails, and the one who is the first to bag a rabbit gets the silver dollar."

Granny tossed the coin into the air and the boys watched as it hit the floor.

"It's heads," Kevin yelled and headed for the rifle.

At last Granny had settled the disagreement. The ladies began clearing the table and the male members left for the hunt.

Ida Mae watched as they marched toward the meadow fields, guns in hand and more than a sufficient amount of ammunition in their pockets. That was everyone except Kervin. The only weapon he carried was a slingshot and a small pouch containing several round steel balls from discarded wheel bearings. To most, it might seem that he was at a disadvantage; but Ida Mae knew better. When it came to being able to shoot this primitive weapon, her little brother was a master. He was the best in the county and maybe the whole state. She hoped that one day he would be able to prove it in open competition.

"Don't kill more than you can carry," Mary Ellen called out, "and dinner will be ready by two."

Once the men folk were out of their way, the ladies begin catching up on the latest news while making preparations for their Thanksgiving dinner. Granny began firing questions at Ida Mae so fast that one would have thought she was a news reporter. She asked about everything from life in the city, to how Jake was coming along with his daddy's logging business, and when she was planning to have a baby.

Mary Sue hummed some of the latest country songs as she listened. She smiled at her sister's ability to pacify Granny with the answers she knew would be best suited for her to take to her weekly ladies club meeting. When at last Granny slowed long enough for Ida Mae to change the subject, she directed her attention to Mary Sue.

"John Robert tells me that when you sang on stage with Hank Williams it was hard to tell which of you received the greatest applause. How would you like to sing on stage again, this time by yourself?"

"That would be wonderful, but I would really rather sing with Hank. He is the greatest."

"I'm serious," Ida Mae continued. "One of the biggest talent shows in the South is taking place in Winston the weekend before Christmas. Jake and I think you could be a winner."

"How do I enter?"

"You already are."

"How did that happen?"

"I gave the promoters all your information three weeks ago."

"How am I going to get there?"

We've taken care of that, too."

"We?" Mary Sue turned to her mother who was standing behind her smiling. "You knew about all these arrangements?"

Mary Ellen nodded, smiling with pride in her younger daughter.

Mary Sue slumped into the nearest seat at the kitchen table. She was absolutely without comment.

"We've already begun rooting for you," Granny interjected.

"You knew about this, too?" Mary Sue asked.

"Sure did. Now can I tell the ladies at our next meeting?" She turned to Mary Ellen as if asking for permission.

Everyone seemed shocked. They realized that for the first time Granny had been able to keep a secret!

Ida Mae explained how she and their mother had been making plans for this occasion for weeks. "The tryouts will be on Thursday and Friday; the twelve finalists will compete on stage Saturday night. A band will accompany each contestant who will perform before an audience of about a thousand. Jake is shutting his daddy's business down for the holidays, and he will pick you up on his way to Winston the day before tryouts."

Mary Sue was overjoyed with this unexpected opportunity. She had to go somewhere to be alone for a few moments to let this soak in. She walked to the water table, grabbed a bucket in each hand and sailed off the back porch singing "Your Cheating Heart" as loud as her vocal cords would allow.

"She'll be great," her mother said, "and she will be even more surprised when she sees all of us seated near the stage."

"I think I'll wait until tonight to tell her that first prize is five hundred dollars cash and a five hundred dollar scholarship to the college of the winners choice. I believe she's had all the excitement she can handle for a little while."

The day passed rather quickly; and as mid-afternoon approached, the long kitchen table became burdened with enough food to feed an army. This was good because when the fellows came dragging in from their day's safari, with only one rabbit to show for their labor, they were all starved.

The ladies watched as Kervin tied the day's kill to the limb of the maple tree near the yard gate. He did so to assure that no animal would devour it before it could be skinned and prepared for a delicious meal one day in the future.

"I see you all bagged your limit," Granny teased.

Kervin reminded Granny about the silver dollar as he plunged into the tale about how he had killed the only rabbit they had seen.

"Shut-Up!" Kevin interrupted when the yarn began to unfold.

Kervin was not about to let this story go untold. As it were, the hunting party walked for more than four hours without jumping a single rabbit. They had given up and were almost back home when, as luck would have it, Kevin stumbled upon a furry creature hunkered beneath a thorn bush. Being true sportsmen, no one in the party was going to shoot at the rabbit without giving him a running chance to escape. Kervin tossed a small rock toward the bush while his daddy and two brothers held their fire arms at ready. As the stone hit the bush the rabbit was off and running. Kevin, being the only one to have a clear shot, took careful aim and fired the rifle.

The rabbit acted as if nothing had happened. It kept running in a circle. A moment later it came full speed straight at Kervin who raised his slingshot and let go; the rabbit fell without knowing what had hit him. Kervin started laughing so hard he could hardly speak but he finally managed to say to his twin brother, "Go Get It Deadeye."

"Get it yourself," Kevin growled; "I'm going to the house."

Chapter Seven

A TRIP TO THE CITY

It was Monday morning on the Baxter farm and the joyous holiday weekend was history. Jake and Ida Mae were leaving for their trip back to Winston; and Ira was about to begin his next day's work.

Mary Sue watched as the vehicles went down the long lane to the graveled road. There was an indescribable knot in the pit of her stomach. It was as if they were leaving on a journey that would prevent them from ever having another family reunion. After a moment she realized it was simply a feeling of sadness because the weekend celebration was over.

She would be leaving for school shortly and wondered if she should share her excitement with a few of her closest friends in her Senior Class. No way she decided; she would wait until the show was over. If she did well, she would let everyone know; and if she did poorly, no one need ever know.

She worked feverishly on her class work for the next few weeks, but it was getting more and more difficult to keep her mind off her trip to Winston. There was a multitude of decisions to be made. What should she wear? Which song should she sing? What could she do to impress the judges? Would she be able to sing with the band? She'd only done that one other time and that was at the Starlight.

Mary Ellen kept reassuring her that the only thing she need be concerned with was her singing. "Ida Mae will take care of your attire for the evening; your voice will impress the judges, and the promoters provide the band. The only thing required of you is to sing well enough to bring down the house."

As the time for the tryout grew nearer the whole family became more supportive. Even the twins who'd before taken pleasure in needling began to give her statements of encouragement.

She would have liked to sing one of Hank Williams numbers, but she knew that would not be wise. Almost all of his songs were in the top ten, and every contestant would be likely to choose one of his songs. She rehearsed every song she knew by every entertainer she knew until she settled on the "Honky Tonk Angels" by Kitty Wells. She practiced every waking hour right up to the time to leave. She had become so good; Granny told her even Kitty wouldn't know it wasn't her doing the singing.

* * * * *

The day for the trip to North Carolina finally arrived. It was a beautiful winter afternoon. There was not a cloud in the ocean blue sky but the chill in the air nibbled at the tip of Mary Sue's nose. She paced back and forth on their front porch waiting for Jake to come pick her up. She kept telling herself to settle down, but that did little to calm the butterflies in her stomach. It was getting late, and she had all but given up on Jake when she saw a green Dodge come into view.

It wasn't Jake. It was J.D. Jake had sent him to pick her up. Buyers were coming the next day to inspect Mr. Hurd's lumber mill. The possibility of a huge contract was in the making, and Mr. Hurd was depending on Jake to be able to close the deal.

This arrangement was a surprise, and it took a while for Mary Sue to convince her mother she would be as safe with J.D. as with Jake. After all, she explained, they were brothers, and Jake would never place her in any danger.

At last her mother agreed and in a little while, they were on their way. They had only traveled a short distance when J.D. asked if she would like to drive.

"You mean now?" she asked.

"Why not?"

"I can't believe you would let me drive this car; it's almost brand new."

"You have a driver's permit, right?"

"Sure, for almost two weeks now."

J.D. pulled over at the next wide area beside the road. He walked around to the passenger's side and told her to scoot over. She slid under the wheel and shifted into gear. The Dodge leaped two or three times before beginning to run smoothly.

"The clutch is a little sensitive but you'll get used to it," he explained.

She drove the next several miles without a hitch; but when she got into town she became a little careless. She was hoping some of her classmates might be hanging out and see what she was driving. None of them were anywhere about, but she did recognize Deputy Howard Barton. He was standing near the intersection that had the only traffic light in town. She was not going to miss the opportunity to let someone she knew see her driving this big new machine. She quickly rolled her window down and yelled, "Hi Howie!"

At that very moment the Dodge came to an abrupt stop directly in front of where Officer Barton stood. She had rammed into the back of an old pickup stopped at the traffic signal.

"Are the brakes a little sensitive too?" she asked.

"I wouldn't know, you never touched them," he stammered.

"Are you alright, you are as pale as a ghost?"

"Fine."

"Then let me handle this."

"Before either of them could make any further comment Barton was standing beside the Dodge. He quickly surveyed the situation determining that none of the parties involved were injured, and the vehicle damage was minor.

"It was all her fault; I was stopped for the light," the old gentleman who was driving the pickup started to explain.

"That's right, but he stopped when the light was green," Mary Sue was quick to offer her side of the story.

"I never stop when the light is green," the gentleman began to argue.

"You're stopped now, and the light is green," the officer stated pointing to the signal. "Better beat it before it turns red."

The old man got back into the pickup and drove off without further comment.

"You're Jake's brother aren't you?" Barton questioned.

J.D. only nodded.

"This your Dodge?"

J.D. nodded again indicating he was correct.

"Might think about getting yourself another driver." He smiled.

"Thanks Howie, I'll tell Daddy you said hello."

"Boy! That was close," J.D. said, his voice quivering.

"You want to drive now?"

J.D. shook his head. "Just be careful."

"Then here goes." Mary Sue gunned the Dodge and sped out of town.

She drove for the next two hours. It was almost dusk dark when she crossed the North Carolina state line. She rounded the first bend in the highway and was surprised by a host of flashing red lights up ahead.

"A bad accident I hope!" J.D. snapped

That was morbid comment she started to say, but a North Carolina Highway Patrolman was beside the Dodge before she had time to speak.

"May I see your driver's license, Miss?"

Mary Sue proudly produced her newly acquired permit.

Jim Campbell

The officer examined the document, returned it to her and shined his flashlight into the back seat. "We've received word there's illegal whiskey headed our way, so we're checking everything crossing the line. You wouldn't mind if I take a look in your trunk?"

"Not at all," She extracted the keys from the ignition, stepped from the vehicle and started toward the rear of the Dodge. She opened the trunk lid exposing eight tightly packed cardboard boxes. The officer opened one of the boxes with his pocketknife and six one-gallon containers of clear liquid came into view.

Mary Sue almost fainted. She knew in an instant what it was she was hauling.

"Please turn around and put you hands behind your back, young lady; you're under arrest."

The patrolman signaled for another officer to take J.D. into custody. He placed Mary Sue into the back seat of his police car while the other officer placed cuffs on J.D. and escorted him to a separate vehicle. She sat trembling and listening to the officer contacting his dispatcher.

"We have two perpetrators in custody, one male, one female and enough white liquor to keep everybody in Surry County drunk for a month. We'll need a tow-truck at this location," he continued. "It looks as if the county will soon be the proud owner of a new good-looking green Dodge. We'll be bringing these two to our crossbar hotel for the night."

"Ten-Four; we'll be waiting."

An hour later they were in Mt. Airy city jail being booked and fingerprinted.

After she had time to really consider what had happened, she became too angry to be nervous. The events of the evening began to fall into place. Now, she knew why J.D. was so willing for her to do the driving and why he thought the fender-bender several miles back was such a close call. She wished she and J.D. could have been transported in the same cruiser so she could also have been arrested for assault. It would do little to add to her sentence

58

she reasoned. She would probably be taken directly to the old folks home when she got out as it were.

The arresting officer didn't say a word until he led her into the sheriff's office. He released her from the handcuffs and stood her in front of a large oak desk. Behind the desk sat a middle-aged, grossly overweight gentleman whose head was as bald as a peeled onion. Deep wrinkles creased his forehead, and his eyes looked as if they belonged to someone twice his size. The officer placed a sheet of paper on the desk in front of the man. "This feller is our Magistrate," he explained.

The Magistrate read the paper in front of him then slipped his horn-rimmed glasses to the very end of his nose. Mary Sue wanted desperately to tell him that he reminded her of a large bullfrog but decided she was in enough trouble already. Instead, she kept silent; but she could not help smiling at the thought.

"This is a serious charge, young lady. Have you anything to say for yourself?" he growled.

"I'm stupid," she blurted.

"That seems to be a true enough statement, anything else?"

"Yes, I would like to make a phone call." Mary Sue knew little about law enforcement, but she did remember hearing her daddy say every prisoner was entitled to one phone call.

The Magistrate raised the receiver from the desk phone. "I'll get your party on the line Missy. What's the number?"

Mary Sue rattled off some numbers and he began dialing. She was standing close enough to hear the phone on the other end ringing. It a moment a rough male voice answered, "Sheriff's Office, Sheriff Baxter speaking."

She was surprised the sheriff was in his office.

The old man's frog eyes widened, "Are you sure you gave me the right number, Missy?"

By this time, she had decided Baxter and her daddy could get her out of this mess; after all they would know she was innocent.

"If you got the sheriff's office, I did."

The Magistrate handed her the phone and listened as she explained the predicament she was in. "I need you to have Daddy send someone down to . . . " She turned to the officer and asked, "Where am I?" The officer gave her the name of the town, and she repeated it to Baxter. "Please ask him to send enough money to bail me out of here."

"How much?" Baxter wanted to know.

"Just a moment." She turned to the old man who was clinging to every word and asked, "How much is my bond?"

The Magistrate leaned back in his chair, pulled his glasses to the end of his nose one more time and said with authority, "Ten thousand dollars sounds about right."

Mary Sue dropped the phone. "Ten thousand dollars," she yelled. Suddenly Mr. Frogeyes didn't strike her as being as funny as before.

"Are you there? Are you there?" Baxter kept repeating.

She finally collected her thoughts, picked up the phone, took a long deep breath and placed the mouthpiece to her lips. "I'm here, sheriff, and from what I'm hearing it appears I'm likely to be a permanent resident."

"Calm down," he told her. "I'll see if I can contact your daddy on the police radio. I've had him out looking for moonshine runners; but," a short pause followed, "it appears you fellows slipped right by him. HANG ON."

She heard him click the talk button on the police base unit. "Deputy Duncan it appears you have an important matter requiring your immediate attention. Report to my office right away, sir."

"Tell him I'll call him back," she said and hung up.

She handed the receiver back to the Magistrate who was shaking his head. "Not tonight you won't, Missy; we're not operating a switchboard at this establishment. Take her to our finest suite, the one that doesn't offer room service," he instructed the arresting officer.

Five minutes later, the sound of doom echoed in her ears as a steel door slammed behind her.

* * * * *

Mary Sue sat in her cell for what seemed like hours. She rehearsed in her mind all the horrible things she would do to J.D. once she was released. How could she have been so stupid?

Sometime after mid-night she stretched her tired frustrated body on the cot in the corner of her cell. The bed reminded her of the slats in the porch swing back on the farm. Her mind drifted back to the farm and how her folks would take the news of her being in jail. What would this do to her plans for being in Winston with Ida Mae? For the first time, she realized what her older sister meant when she tried to tell her how easily it was to be led down the wrong path.

Shortly before dawn, an officer whom she had not seen before unlocked her cell.

He escorted her into the sheriff's office where her daddy, Mr. Hurd, Jake and Ida Mae were waiting. A moment later Mr. Frog-eyes joined them.

"You're free to go, Missy, as soon as you sign this paper promising to appear in court with your friend for the trial."

She hurriedly took the pen and signed the paper. "Word travels fast," she smiled, an expression of relief crossing her face.

Ida Mae was the first to speak. She explained that J.D. used his one phone call to call his father. "Jake had just closed the lumber deal with some big wheels from a furniture factory. His father received a fairly large sum of cash up front. They immediately contacted Daddy, and they drove down together, in separate automobiles of course. Jake called me and I insisted I should meet them here this morning. Mr. Hurd posted bond and is waiting for the officer to bring J.D. from his cell. Let's go eat; I'll bet you're starved."

Mr. Hurd offered his deepest apology as Jake, Ira and his two daughters left the jail. They ate breakfast at a roadside diner just out of town and talked about the events leading up to Mary Sue's arrest.

"How are the folks back home taking it?" Mary Sue wanted to know.

"Your mother is worried sick; the twins think it's marvelous to have a sister who is an outlaw, and Granny is sure she is going to be the star of her next women's club meeting."

"What about Baxter?"

"To be quite honest, he's not happy at all, said we would discuss the matter when I got back to the office."

"I'm sorry Daddy."

"It'll be alright," he assured her. "Jake you drive these gals on down to Winston. There's some rehearsing to do for a talent show, if I recall. I have to get back and try to explain all this to the boss."

Chapter Eight

THE TALENT SHOW

They were barely out of the restaurant parking lot when Ida Mae lit into Jake like a game rooster at a cockfight. She was so angry her voice was trembling. "Let's hear it, Big Boy," she demanded.

Mary Sue sat in the back seat without opening her mouth. In all the years growing up with her older sister she had never seen her display so much fury.

Jake remained calm as his wife lashed out at him. He waited until she finally quieted down long enough for him to speak without fear of being physically attacked.

"Let me explain," he said as he looked into the rear view mirror at Mary Sue who was scrunched into one corner. It was evident that he was about to say what he would have preferred to say in private.

"I'm listening; and this had better be the best yarn you have ever spun!" she told him.

"Well, it's like this," he began. "J.D. left home as soon as he was old enough to quit school, as you already know. He never cared much for the logging business so he headed to Detroit and landed a pretty good job in one of those big GM assembly plants.

He was making more money than he ever dreamed possible but the word *save* was never in his vocabulary. He worked hard all week, and he drank and partied just as hard on weekends."

Mary Sue sat quietly listening to every word. That son-of-a-gun lied to me about where he was from as well as having the new car paid for and who knows what else, she wondered. He had sure better start telling the truth when he explains to the judge about my involvement with his whiskey. If he doesn't he'll get a lesson in telling the truth from the Duncan sisters.

"At the beginning of summer, he decided to purchase a new Dodge at the reduced price made available only to employees. He paid very little down and financed the balance. He immediately brought the Dodge to Winston to have it modified. He had some fool idea of getting into racing. He thought he could win enough money to pay for the Dodge and go into that business full-time. Two months later, he was laid off."

"A tragic story," Ida Mae interrupted. "What's that have to do with the crisis at hand?"

"When two payments were past due, he came home and talked our daddy into helping him pay for the Dodge. He knew our parents had no money and the logging business was at a virtual stand still. He also knew Daddy was friends with all the best moonshiners in the territory and that they needed drivers brave enough to haul their product out of state. After days of persuasion Daddy agreed to tell J.D. who some of them were if he promised to stop once the Dodge was paid for. Neither Mom nor I knew anything about any of this, I swear. J.D. worked long hours during the week helping with the logging business. Every Friday evening, he left the mountain for Winston under the pretence of seeing his girlfriend. I knew nothing about the whiskey until J.D. called from the jail here in North Carolina. Believe me, I am as shocked to learn of this mess as you are."

"How did Sis come to get involved?" Ida Mae asked, her voice not nearly as harsh as before.

"Quite by accident. I was obligated to meet a group of timber buyers so J.D. offered to bring Mary Sue down here while I tried to close a sale. He thought he was doing us a favor. He all but insisted she drive his Dodge because he felt she would be much less likely to get stopped. She was willing to do so, but she had absolutely no knowledge of what she was hauling."

"That's right," Mary Sue added.

"Let's hope we are able to convince the judge," Ida Mae sighed.

"Daddy filled me in on all the details on the way down. By the way, most of the down payment from the lumber deal was used for bail. He felt responsible because he helped J.D. get involved."

By the time Jake was finished explaining the events of the previous two days the Winston city limit sign was coming into view. Ten minutes later, they were sitting in the driveway on Chestnut Street.

"We'll go in and show Mary Sue our home and see if there are any chores you need to do."

"I need to do?"

"Sure! Sis and I are going shopping. I am sorry I blamed you for something you knew nothing about, Honey," she added.

"You can give me a formal apology later." He winked at her and followed the two ladies inside.

* * * * *

It was five hours before talent show tryouts were to begin and the ladies weren't going to allow any of this time to be wasted. They hit the streets of Winston shopping for all the items Mary Sue needed to appear on stage. They went from one ladies' shop to another until they were certain they had found the right garment: a dress much like the one Kitty Wells was pictured wearing on the cover of her latest album.

"Perfect," Ida Mae declared. "If you are going to sing like Kitty, you might just as well look like her."

They arrived at the theatre downtown just as the contestants were starting to receive information about the contest. A hundred or more contestants filled seats near the front of the stage. A variety of musical instruments were leaning against the walls or lying in seats nearby. Half-dozen neatly dressed folks with pens and note-books sat near the back of the theatre. Mary Sue would later learn these were the judges.

In a short while, a middle-aged lady walked on stage. She introduced herself and thanked each contestant who had signed up to display his or her talent.

"There are eighty performances to be judged," she stated. "Half of you will perform tonight; the remainder, tomorrow night. You will be selected in alphabetical order so please be ready when called. And, be aware that only twenty acts will be chosen to go on to Saturday night's grand finale. The twenty finalists will be announced when the tryouts close tomorrow evening. When per-forming Saturday night, you will be accompanied by one of the South's most popular bands. Now, let us begin and good luck to each of you."

Each act took its turn. Some were good; some, very good and a few Mary Sue felt embarrassed for. Many sang songs that had been recorded by popular entertainers, but none sang any of Kitty Well's tunes. When at last her turn came, Mary Sue walked onto the stage. As she passed the band she instructed the lead guitar player to please do an intro into "Honky Tonk Angels" in the key of G.

She had never sung in competition before; and during the first verse she was aware the judges could tell she was nervous. She looked to her sister for any type of encouragement. Ida Mae raised her hands, palms up, indicating she should let go. This was exactly what Mary Sue needed. She closed her eyes and began singing as she did practicing back on the farm. As she finished her number and walked off stage, Ida Mae greeted her with a big hug. "You were great," she whispered.

They stayed until the first evening's tryouts ended and was there to listen to every act the next day. When the final song ended the judges took about half-hour before rendering their decisions. Mary Sue felt confident she had done well, but she also knew she had faced stiff competition. Some of the performers, she had to admit, were really good.

When the lady who was MC for the tryouts came back on stage, Mary Sue's knees begin to shake. "You are all winners," she announced, "but only twenty of you have been chosen as finalists to perform in tomorrow's show. Those twenty will need to stay to receive further instructions and the rest of you may leave."

The lady began reading the names of the contestants chosen by the judges. She did so very slowly as if to keep each in suspense as long as possible. A short applause followed each name; but as the list became longer, more disappointed looks began appearing on the faces of many of the performers. When the number reached nineteen most of the contestants, including Mary Sue, began moving toward the exits. She was almost back to where the judges were seated when she heard her name being announced as one of the finalists.

Mary Sue turned to say something to Ida Mae but was surprised to see she was not following her. She rushed to where she was sitting, "I can't believe I made it," she proclaimed.

"I wouldn't have believed it if you hadn't; I think you will be number one. Think they might let me be one of the judges?" she smiled.

When the lady MC finished instructions for the following evening, the two girls headed back to Chestnut Street and picked up Jake. From there it was downtown to one of the finest restaurants in Winston. After stuffing themselves with all the food they could eat, some Mary Sue could not identify, Jake and Ida Mae gave her a tour of the city. The hustle, bustle, bright lights and busy sidewalks were beyond anything she could have imagined.

It was nearing midnight when the threesome got back to Chestnut Street. A dimly lit porch light made visible a welcome sign that hung over the door. Just inside the entrance foyer was another small plaque that read, ***You May Enter As Strangers Only If You Leave As Friends.*** Beneath the sign sat a small table almost completely covered with unopened mail. Ida Mae picked up most of the items and carried them into the parlor. She placed the mail on a coffee table and instructed Mary Sue to make herself comfortable while she fixed each of them a cup of hot tea. "Jake can sort through the bills while you and I read the good stuff," she smiled as she disappeared into another room.

Mary Sue sat on the end of the sofa near a huge fireplace. The warmth of a flickering fire made the large room feel more than a little inviting. Filled bookcases lined two of the ten-foot high walls and expensive Victorian furniture took most of the floor space. The setting was exactly as her family had described when they visited Sarah during the time Jake and John Robert were recovering from their almost fatal automobile crash.

The sound of people moving in the bedroom overhead indicated there were guests in the house. No different than what Sarah would have done Mary Sue was certain.

Jake, who was seated at the other side of the room, was busy sorting the mail. Ida Mae came back into the parlor carrying a small tray. On the tray was a beautifully decorated pitcher of steaming hot mint tea and three matching cups.

Ida Mae poured tea for each of them, and Jake disappeared into a small office adjacent to the parlor to take care of the business at hand. She sat beside Mary Sue, placed a stack of letters on her lap and handed her a sharp pointed letter opener. She leaned back, slipped off her slippers, placed her heels on the coffee table, and asked if she would mind to read some of the letters.

Mary Sue opened the first envelope and unfolded the letter. A twenty-dollar bill fell onto her lap. A few words expressing appreciation of kindness made up the contents of the letter. She read almost two-dozen letters; half of them contained checks or small amounts of cash but every one contained words of gratitude.

"Just like it was when Sarah lived here," she said. When Ida Mae did not answer she turned to discover she was sound asleep. Mary Sue curled up on the other end of the sofa and slept the night away.

When she awoke the next day, it took a moment to realize she was not in her own room. The thoughts of the previous couple of days came racing back. It was as if they were part of a bad dream. She was about to become overtaken with awful thoughts of things she would like to do to J.D. when Ida Mae came into the parlor.

"Time to get ready for breakfast, Sis; we have a busy day ahead of us, remember."

Mary Sue went into a nearby bathroom, splashed cold water on her face, and ran her sister's comb through hair that looked as if it hadn't been combed in days. The results of bad dreams, she determined. When she considered herself halfway presentable, she went into the dining room. Ida Mae and a lady whom she did not know were busy carrying food from the kitchen and placing it on the dining room table. Jake and a gentleman whom she assumed to be the lady's husband were seated at one end of the table discussing an article in the newspaper. Ida Mae later learned they were the guests she heard in the upstairs bedroom the night before.

When they finished eating, the guests insisted the two sisters get started with their day and leave the cleaning up to them. Unlike most days, Ida Mae welcomed their offer.

The ladies disappeared into a different part of the house and reappeared an hour later looking as if they had just stepped out of a beauty parlor. Ida Mae put a record on the phonograph, and Kitty Wells voice filled the air. "Thought you might want to listen to Kitty sing for a while."

"Thanks, Sis. You're all right."

Jake brought a box into the parlor and placed it on the coffee table. "This is for you, Mary Sue," he said.

Mary Sue opened the box to find a state of the art, reel-to-reel tape recorder.

She could not contain her excitement, "Show me how to make it work," she begged.

Jake placed the reels on the spindles, plugged in the mike and turned on the machine. "Push this button, and you're ready to go."

For the next few hours, Mary Sue did nothing but practice. Record and play; record and play. She kept asking Ida Mae to offer constructive criticism, but her sister refused. "You'll be the envy of half the contestants and will win the hearts of the entire audience."

"What about the judges?"

"Jake and I think you're great, and I thought we were the only ones who mattered," she teased.

When it was at last time to leave, Mary Sue came into the parlor where Jake and Ida Mae were waiting. Her new dress could not have fit more perfectly if it had been tailor-made. The new pair of ladies' white western boots made her to appear a full two inches taller. Her jet-black hair, inherited from her daddy, fell gently about her shoulders and the faint glow of rose pink lipstick made her smile look more radiant.

"You'll be a winner even if no one hears you sing," Jake smiled.

When they reached the auditorium, people were lined up at the ticket booth. Mary Sue presented her pass, and they were allowed to go in. Several seats in front of the stage were reserved for family members. Jake and Ida Mae took seats in this area, and Mary Sue disappeared behind the curtain. A band hidden back stage played hits by the latest recording artists while each contestant drew a number from a box to determine in what order he or she would perform.

Thirty minutes later, the auditorium became dark. The band ceased playing and a large spotlight hit center stage. A gentleman in a tuxedo stepped from behind the curtain and welcomed the audience. He introduced the judges and announced the name of the band. Applause followed the announcement of the band, so Mary Sue supposed they must be very good and very well known.

"They have been presented with the name of each song the contestants will sing and are well practiced." When the applause died down, the announcer continued. "There will be two segments of tonight's contest. Each contestant will sing a number of his or her choice during the first segment. When all twenty of the contestants have sung, there will be a twenty-minute intermission. The band will entertain during intermission; they are accompanying the contestants without pay so please show them your appreciation. The second segment will be the same, except the performers will sing a different number of the judges' choice and will sing in reverse order. We have some great talent for your enjoyment, so let us begin."

Each contestant took his or her turn, and each seemed better than the one before. At the end of each number the spotlight drifted to the family section so the contestant could see their reactions. The whistles and applause from the audience were proof that the judges, during the tryouts, had done their jobs well. Near the end of the first segment, the announcer stepped to the center stage to announce the next contestant. He introduced each in like manner. "And next is Miss Mary Sue Duncan from the hills of Virginia."

She walked to center stage and the spotlight all but blinded her. She could not see Jake and Ida Mae, but she could sense they were in the midst of a packed house. The band knew what her first number was so they played the introduction to "Honky Tonk Angels," and Miss Duncan began to sing, as she had never done before.

At the beginning of the second verse the whistles from the audience began. She felt more at ease at the thought of knowing she was doing well. Near the last words of her song, the spotlight hit the family section; and she almost hit the floor. Every member of her family was on their feet. Her parents, Jake, Ida Mae and John Robert led the applause; and Granny and the twins were doing more their share of the whistling.

When her song ended, she managed to make it off stage without her knees folding. She could hardly believe the response from the audience and was thrilled beyond measure to have her family leading her cheering section. She felt she had performed well, but she also knew some of the other contestants had done equally as well. She sat back stage and waited for the first round to come to an end. The moment it did, she bounded offstage to greet the leading members of her fan club. She was simply amazed to learn they had begun planning to attend weeks ago and more amazed that they were all able to keep it from her. She received hugs, compliments, and words of encouragement from each of them and more from people she did not know. Her visit was cut short as the lights above the audience began to dim, and the announcer walked back onto the stage.

"What are you going to sing next?" Kervin asked hurriedly.

"Only the announcer, the band and I know," she whispered.

"Then go knock'em dead, Sis," he said as she disappeared into the darkness.

The final segment of the show began much like the first except most of the contestants now seemed more relaxed. Stage fright was not nearly as evident so most of them did much better than they had earlier.

Many of the performers were really good, and the audience was getting more excited. They were becoming more supportive of their favorite performer as they did their final number. She was glad she was one of the acts instead of one of the judges. She really wanted to place near the top but decided that whoever won would be very deserving.

When it was again her turn the announcer introduced her and introduced her next number as "Your Cheating Heart" written by the great Hank Williams.

The audience started applauding before the band played the first note.

As nervous as she was, she knew this was to be her chance to let her real talents show. Win or lose, she was determined to make her family proud. As she began singing the chorus for the last time, she was sure she had accomplished her goal. The applause was almost deafening, and the crowd was coming to its feet. She had no idea if she would win but she was confident she had done her best. After the applause ended for the final contestant, a hush fell over the audience.

She, like every one else in the building could hardly wait for the decision of the judges.

When at last the results were handed to the announcer, he came into the spotlight near center stage. The twenty performers were standing in a half-circle behind him awaiting the outcome. "Before I recognize the winners," he began, "I have a very important announcement. A representative for one of the leading recording studios in Nashville, Tennessee, is in our audience and would like to meet with tonight's winner to discuss the possibility of a recording contract. None of the contestants knew of his presence, but he has been seated front row center during the entire show." The spotlight focused on the representative as he was being announced, and both the audience and the contestants gave him a generous applause.

"And in conclusion let me add. To avoid any resemblance of showing favoritism none of the contestants had met the members of the band. Let me introduce them at this time." As he made this announcement, the backstage curtain slid open; and the band came into view. Standing front and center, with guitar in hand, stood the young soldier she had met at the Starlight. Mary Sue almost went into shock; and for the next few minutes, she did not hear a word that was being spoken.

She returned to reality as the announcer was saying, "And now for the moment we have all been waiting for. The third place winner is Miss Rita Smith from the beautiful state of Kentucky." After hesitating until Miss Smith received her much deserved applause he continued. "Second place goes to Mr. Jerry McGuire who hails from the sunshine state of Florida." He waited until he too received an enormous round of applause before stepping back to the microphone. "And now ladies and gentlemen, let's hear it for our first place winner from the hills of Virginia, Miss Mary Sue Duncan."

The audience once more came to their feet and began crying out for more. Mary Sue walked to center stage and motioned for the guitar player to join her. Eddie stepped to her side; and as they began singing "I'm So Lonesome I Could Cry" the crowd went wild.

When their song ended and the applause ended the announcer presented Mary Sue with five new hundred-dollar bills and a voucher for five hundred dollars to a college of her choice. Other contestants offering congratulations and extending well wishes surrounded her. She thanked the announcer, the judges, the audience, and a special thanks to her family. She shuffled through the crowd to where they were waiting. They greeted her with hugs and kisses and much-deserved compliments. She had most surely made every one of them proud.

A tall well-dressed gentleman came to where the family was gathered. He shook hands with Mary Sue and reached her his business card. "I'm Shawn Ross, the studio representative your announcer spoke about. I must say you were good, correction, you were marvelous, Miss Duncan. I realize you are much too caught up in the happenings of the evening to talk business, but please me you will give me a call after the holidays. I think you have a great future in the world of entertaining," he concluded.

Mary Sue thanked him, promised she would call and turned to her family. "Let's get out of here before I get the big head," she smiled.

"Forget about having a big head; let's go cash that big check," Kervin suggested.

"Later, little brother; I'm beat. Let's go somewhere where we can rest."

They left downtown and drove to Jake and Ida's Mae home on Chestnut Street. Ida Mae led the way to the front porch; and as she opened the door, the smell of food got everyone's attention. A pitcher of hot coffee, one with tea, and a platter piled high with a variety of sandwiches welcomed the family to their dining room table. The lady and her husband, who were Jake and Ida Mae's guests, had promised to have a bite to eat ready after the show; and boy, had they fulfilled their promise.

The family dived in as Ida Mae hoped they would. Mary Sue was seated beside her daddy, sipping her tea but paying little attention to what was being said. She was overwhelmed with the events of the evening, but she could no longer hide her worries about the happenings in Mt. Airy.

"What will they do to me, Daddy?" she asked. She spoke as if she had suddenly awakened from a bad dream. Her frightened tone of voice got everyone's attention, and the room went completely silent. Ira looked puzzled for a moment as if trying to think of something to say to assure her everything would be all right. He had succeeded at this many times when she was a little tot suffering from a bee sting or a mashed finger. Suddenly he realized she was no longer a little girl but a grown woman facing a serious dilemma.

He placed one arm around her shoulders, pulled her closer, and spoke in a voice as comforting as he could muster. "I'll take care of things on the way home Monday morning. We all know you're innocent; and with all the luck you're having, how could anything go wrong?"

* * * * *

Ira was the first member of the Duncan family to get out of bed the following morning. He walked quietly down the stairs and onto the front porch. He had spent a restless night wondering what he could do to keep his promise to Mary Sue. Not only did his daughter face jail time for a crime she did not commit, he faced problems back home. His boss had given him strict orders to get this matter settled at once and make sure news of the incident did not get back to Virginia.

He sat quietly, listening to the sounds of the city. Much unlike the sounds of a Sunday morning back in the mountains, he reasoned. The sounds of a barking dog, a rooster crowing, or the ringing of a church bell were replaced with those of fast moving automobiles, sirens, and planes landing or becoming airborne.

Chestnut Street was one of the most serene places in the city. It was tucked away in the southern end of town, lined on either side with maple trees that shaded homes occupied, for the most part, by folks living in their sunset years.

He was happy for Ida Mae and Jake, but he was convinced he would not trade country life for life in the city. He was about to become lost in his thoughts of comparing different lifestyles, when he saw someone approaching. He recognized the gentleman as the one who was helping in the dining room the evening before. "May I join you?" he asked.

"Certainly. You're out early."

"I am an early riser," he began as he sat down in a rocking chair beside Ira. "Got used to it growing up on a farm. I like to keep up with the happenings in the world so I stroll down to the corner drug store for a newspaper as soon as I get out of bed. Been doing that for the last two months now."

"You've been here for two months?"

"Yes sir, ever since the accident."

"Accident?"

"Didn't your daughter tell you?"

"No, sir, she says little concerning her guests and we never pry."

"Then let me explain what happened," he began. "I grew up on a dairy farm in Eastern Kentucky. Married the girl next door, built us a home, and raised us a daughter. We've been together almost forty years now. Never been very far from home and never wanted to be. Couldn't go far now if we did. It takes most everything we make just to keep the farm going."

"Then, why are you here in Winston?"

76

"I was getting to that," he continued. "Our girl finished high school, in the top of her class, and got the notion she wanted to be a doctor. She enrolled in college here in North Carolina and moved into a very small apartment. Several months later she starts going with this young man from somewhere up near Mt. Airy. Anyway, they made up their minds they were going to get married. So, what can you do? You know how young folks are these days; if they decide they are going to do something you might as well go along. Me and Liddy were going to borrow enough money to give her a big wedding, but she would have no part of that. It was just his parents, her mother and I, a few close friends, and the preacher. They got married right there on the farm in Kentucky.

"They left right after the wedding on their honeymoon for a rented cabin up in the mountains. Going to spend two weeks living like early settlers, I suppose. Anyway the second day they were there my son-in-law had a bad accident with a chain saw that caused him to almost lose a leg. He's been in the hospital here in Winston for nigh on to two months. I don't know what we would have done if it hadn't been for that girl of yours and her husband. They've been like family to us. Anyway, the doctors say he can go home in another day or two so I guess me and the missus will head on back to Kentucky.

"He's says he wants to be a doctor, too; but I can't figure that happening. He has a brother who just finished law school and his daddy is a judge. They'll probably settle down here in North Carolina when they finish college. That probably will be the end of her living on the dairy farm."

All of a sudden ideas started spinning around in Ira's head like a pea in a whistle. He stopped rocking, leaned his chair forward, and placed a hand on the old fellows shoulder. "I'm Ira Duncan, Ida Mae's Daddy; it was so late when we got here last night we didn't get formally introduced."

The old gentleman patted the hand that lay on his shoulder. "I'm Ezra Snider, but most folks back home just call me Ez".

"Well it sure is good to make your acquaintance, Mr. Snider. Now where did you say your son-in-law's family lived?"

"Mt. Airy."

"Well, ain't that a coincidence? It just so happens I have to stop in Mt. Airy on my way back home tomorrow, police business you know."

"Why, that's right, your girl did tell us you was a sheriff."

"Just a deputy, Mr. Snider. What is the young fellow's name, your son-in-law, I mean."

"Robert Wallace; but Gracie, that's our daughter, she calls him Bobby."

Ida Mae came out onto the porch, "Would you fellows like a cup of coffee while you wait for breakfast?"

"That would be great, Darling; but I'll come and get it. Can I bring you anything else, Mr. Snider?" he asked.

A few moments earlier Ira had no thought of food; but suddenly he had acquired a ravishing appetite. He had dreaded his visit back to Mt. Airy; but after his conversation with Ezra, he felt things might not be as bad as they'd seemed. The thought foremost on his mind now was to get back to Surry County and find an attorney who was in good standing with the Honorable Judge William F. Wallace, Sr.

CHAPTER NINE

MISDIRECTED TRUST

The Duncan family rushed through breakfast and hit the streets of Winston. It was their last day before leaving for home and Jake and Ida Mae were taking them on a tour of the city. Jake chauffeured the men folk in John Robert's Chevy and Ida Mae followed driving her own car with all the ladies aboard. They drove downtown and strolled the streets for more than three hours. Since it was Sunday most of the businesses were closed, but window-shopping was a delightful treat. The chill of winter, decorations in store windows, and Christmas music echoing through the streets were enough to erase the cares of the last few days, at least for the moment.

Lunch was a sack full of hot dogs, potato chips, and bottled soft drinks purchased from a street-corner vendor. Then, it was off to the city park for a short period of relaxation. Ida Mae hoped the park would be fun for the twins, but they were not as impressed as she had hoped. Sleighs made of cardboard sliding on broom sage on the hills back home were much longer and faster than those in the park. And, the swings couldn't compare with the lengthy grapevines hanging from the tops of the huge oak and hickory trees back in the mountains.

The real treat for Granny and the twins was the matinee at the Grand Theatre on Main Street. A western featuring Johnny Mac Brown and Fuzzy Jones kept the twins' eyes glued to the screen. And Granny, who was well into her sixties, had never witnessed anything so amazing. "I can't wait to tell the ladies about our trip to North Carolina," she said as they were leaving the theatre.

"Just make sure you leave out the part about Surry County," Ira cautioned.

"Is there any thing any of you would like to do before we call it a day?" Jake asked.

"Just one more," Ira answered. "I would like to stop by the hospital to visit Mr. Snider's son-in-law."

Ida Mae smiled as if she were reading his mind. "Jake will be happy to drive you over; the rest of us will go on home."

* * * * *

Jake pulled to the front entrance of the hospital. "I'll be waiting for you in the car," he told his father-in-law. He was well aware of the purpose of Ira's hospital visit, and he also knew he would want to handle it in his own way.

"Thanks, Son," he said. "I won't be long."

Jake was proud of himself for the manner in which he was handling the situation; and he was certain Ira was, too, because it was the first time he had ever called him *son*. He watched as his father-in-law walked through the glass door, stopped for a moment at the information desk, and then disappeared. He knew he would have no trouble finding his way around. Ira had spent so much time in this place while Jake and John Robert were hospitalized; he knew many of the staff by their first name.

As Ira stepped from the elevator, he recalled the many times he had done so several months before. He walked past a small family waiting room where he had spent many hours praying that Jake and John Robert would not slip into the Great Beyond. A few steps down the corridor, he reached his destination. He stopped for a moment contemplating what method to use to tactfully acquire the information he needed. "Just come right out with it," he decided and slowly opened the door.

"That was by far the most hilarious excuse for a defense I had ever heard; I couldn't decide if I should punish the defendant or his attorney," someone said. Outbursts of laughter followed. Ira was about to turn to leave, thinking he must have the wrong room just as a young lady acknowledged his presence.

"May I help you, sir?" She asked.

"I guess not," he was quick to answer, "I was looking for Mr. William Wallace."

"Junior or Senior? Oh, it doesn't matter; they're both here, come on in."

Ira stepped into the crowded room and introduced himself.

The lady jumped from her chair and rushed to his side. "I'm Gracie Snider, I mean Wallace," she corrected herself, looking embarrassed. "You're Ida Mae's father; please come in. I want you to meet my husband and his family. This is my mother and father-in-law Mr. and Mrs. William Wallace, Sr., my husband Bobby, and his brother, William Jr. I guess you could say we're celebrating, Bobby is going home tomorrow."

The Wallace family spent the next ten minutes expressing their gratitude for Ida Mae's kindness to Gracie's parents. Ira told them his daughter had talked so much about the newlyweds he felt he could not leave town until he made their acquaintance. He stayed just long enough to be polite and not long enough to be a nuisance. As he bid them farewell, he felt relieved; he had gained information he needed without revealing the true purpose of his visit. Gracie followed him into the hall and assured him that if there was ever anything her family could do to repay Jake and Ida Mae's hospitality, all they need do was ask

"If she only knew," he thought as the he made his way to the parking lot where Jake was waiting. It was not until the next day that he discovered how much help the Duncan family would really need.

Monday morning the Duncan family headed north out of Winston. Mary Ellen, Granny, Jake, and the twins traveled with John Robert in his Chevy heading for home in the mountains. Mary Sue and Ira followed as far as Surry County in a loaner he'd borrowed from the county. She had an appointment with the Magistrate at ten in the morning, and he'd already cautioned her not to be late. He had not kept her locked-up over the weekend as a favor to her daddy because, he too, was in law enforcement; but, nonetheless, he intended for her to know he was in charge.

Ira promised he would have her there promptly at ten, and he had kept his word. It was, in fact, a quarter before ten when they walked into the jail. They took a seat on the bench outside the Magistrate's office and waited for over an hour. The longer they waited the angrier Mary Sue became. She insisted Old Frogeyes was intentionally being late just to antagonize her and Ira thought she might be right until he came rushing into the jail carrying a folder under his arm. He unlocked his office door and motioned for them to follow him inside. "Sorry I'm late," he said. "I've been talking with the court clerk. We have your preliminary hearing set for four months from today on April 22nd. I suggest you get yourself a very good attorney, Missy; hauling illegal whiskey across state lines is a very serious crime."

"Any you recommend?" Ira questioned.

The Magistrate pulled a phone directory out of a drawer and slid it across the top of the desk.

Ira searched the yellow pages until he found a law firm with the name Wallace. He wrote the name, address, and phone number on a scratch pad and walked out of the office to where a couple of uniformed officers were seated on the bench where he and Mary Sue had set earlier.

Ira introduced himself and his daughter and asked directions to the address he had just written. The younger of the two officers was more than glad to be of assistance. He led them into another office where a large city map hung on the wall. Ira's eyes searched the map while the young officer's eyes remained glued on Mary Sue. "This is it," he said pointing to a spot on the map. "Nothing much on that block but lawyers, offices" he volunteered.

Mary Sue was fully aware of his eagerness to help. "Any you know?" she asked.

"One or two, personally I mean."

"What about Smith, Donnelly, and Wallace?" Ira asked.

"Best in the city, especially Lawyer Wallace. He's young, ambitious, and always gives a 100 percent to his clients. I think he will run for prosecuting attorney someday, probably be elected too. His daddy is one of our Circuit Court Judges, you know."

"Is that right?" Mary Sue asked. "You've been most helpful. Is there a phone my daddy could use?"

"Right here," the officer said without hesitation.

Ira tried several times to reach the number to the attorney's office; but each time, the line was busy. All the while the young police officer was trying to learn as much as he could about Mary Sue. She told him as little as possible without being rude, but she certainly did not tell him she was the one in need of an attorney.

After a few more tries, Ira turned to her, "Mr. Wallace is extremely busy today, but we have an appointment in two weeks."

"Then are we ready to leave?"

"On our way," Ira answered.

Mary Sue was glad to make their exit. The young officer seemed really nice and had been most helpful. All the more reason she wanted to leave before he became aware that she was an outlaw.

They did not discuss legal matters during the remainder of their trip home. They talked only of her performance at the talent show. She had exceeded all expectations and she deserved this time to celebrate. Ira was not going to see her accomplishments overshadowed with worry about legal matters. After all, he felt he had made enough contacts to most likely have all charges against her dropped. If only he could get back to Mt. Airy and have this matter resolved before the news reached home.

All he wanted at this time was to get back to the mountains. Suddenly, he felt like a lost, scared child surrounded by strange events being controlled by even stranger people. Although law enforcement was never easy, he felt that as an officer in his own county he was in command. He became more and more relieved as the miles rolled by and his beloved mountains came closer and closer. He needed to return the borrowed car to the county garage, convince Baxter of his daughter's innocence, and forget about the events of the last few days. He had become so lost in his thoughts he had not noticed his daughter's silence. He turned to her and started to speak, but her limp body was slumped against the passenger's door enjoying a period of peaceful rest she so badly needed. He smiled at her and thought of how beautiful she would look someday standing on stage at the Grand Ole Opry. She never moved until he stopped the car in front of their home.

Ira breathed a sigh of relief and sat for a moment watching the clouds slowly crown the top of the mountain. He lowered the side glass and felt the first really cold blast of winter wind come rushing in. Tiny droplets of snow started decorating the windshield, displaying their unmatched beauty for a brief instant before giving way to the warmth beneath them. In only three days it would be Christmas. A week later another year would come to an end; and life's cycle for the Duncan family would start anew. It had been a good year he reasoned and he had much to be thankful for. He promised himself he would spend the next few days enjoying the holiday season with his family and worry about unpleasant matters later. And that was exactly what he did.

Most Christmas parties throughout the county were peaceful and calls for disturbances were very limited. The sheriff was supposedly visiting family out of the county and left word with his dispatcher he was to be contacted only in the event of an emergency. These arrangements suited perfectly. He, Howard and the other three deputies worked closely together concerning police matters so each had as much time as possible with their families. Ira took off from work on New Year's Day. John Robert was leaving for the coast the next morning; Mary Sue and the twins would be going back to school and he would begin dealing with the situation in the Carolinas. The holiday season could not have gone better. But, the Duncan family could not have guessed the challenges they would face so soon after the beginning of the New Year.

* * * * *

When Mary Sue stepped from the school bus the next morning half the student body was waiting to greet her. Cries of *"For she's a jolly good fellow"* echoed through the crowd. She had rapidly become a celebrity. Even the principal told her she was putting Russellville High on the map.

"How did you find out?" she asked.

"Good new travels fast," someone shouted.

"I wonder how they will react if they get word of the bad news," she thought. She determined she wasn't going to worry about that now; she was going to allow herself to enjoy the thrill of the moment. Very little class work was discussed during the entire day. Students and teachers alike were full of questions about the talent show. Questions such as: What was she going to do with the money? Was she still planning to attend college? What about the recording studio? And the questions went on and on. Students she hardly knew began flocking to her like bees to honey. They treated her as if she had just received her first gold record. The recognition was gratifying, and she enjoyed the attention, but she was determined not to let anything interfere with her education. She more clearly understood the need for good attorneys as a result of the happenings in Surry County. It only deepened her desire to become one of the best. She'd even decided to postpone calling the agent at the recording studio until after the hearing. It wasn't that she didn't appreciate the opportunity to perform in the presence of a group of professionals, she really did. Each day she became more fearful that the moonshining news would reach the school; but by the end of the week, Mary Sue was becoming more relaxed.

Things did not go so well with Ira, however. Baxter was extremely disturbed by all that had taken place. He was by no means convinced Mary Sue knew nothing about the whiskey. But, the thing that really disturbed him most was the embarrassment it might bring on his department.

"How will it look if the people of this county discover that your daughter is a moonshine runner?" he asked.

The sheriff paced the floor as Ira tried to explain how it all came about, but it was to no avail. The conversation came to an end when Baxter announced he was placing Ira on a two-week administrative leave and suggested he use the time to get the matter cleared up.

"Leave your cruiser parked at home so your neighbors will think you're on vacation and say nothing of this to anyone. Keep me informed about what's being done," he demanded.

Ira left the sheriff's office filled with mixed emotions. He was pleased, angry, and totally frustrated. He was pleased to have time off so he could get this mess cleared up as quickly as possible. But he was angry with his boss for believing his daughter might be guilty. He was also frustrated by being so blinded at what the Hurd family was doing right under his nose.

But he felt no animosity toward Jake; he was as shocked as anyone to learn what was going on. In fact, they decided it might be to their advantage if the two parties worked together to get the matter resolved. So, on the morning of the appointment with the attorney, Jake and Ira traveled together to Mt. Airy.

They found the address they were looking for and were greeted by a receptionist as soon as they entered the office. "Are you Mr. Duncan?" she asked.

Ira nodded, indicating he was.

"Mr. Wallace has been awaiting your arrival, follow me please."

She led them down a wide plush carpeted hallway. Large oak-framed, oil-painted portraits of attorneys hung on either wall.

Polished brass plates bearing the name and the number of years with the firm were attached to each frame.

The attorney rose from his desk the moment they entered his office. "Come in, Mr. Duncan," he said. "And let me apologize. My secretary makes all of my appointments, and I did not realize it was you who was on my calendar until earlier today. If I had known I would have seen you days ago. Now that you're here, how may I help you sir?"

Ira introduced Jake and for the remainder of the morning he and Jake explained the need for his services. Jake told him of his family's past participation in the moonshining business. He even told of his personal involvement that led to the automobile crash that rendered him crippled. The young attorney was fascinated at what he was hearing. He hung on to every word as intently as if he were a wee tot hearing the story of the three bears for the first time. He'd met Ida Mae on more than one occasion while visiting his brother in the hospital. He knew his sister-in-law's parents lived in her home temporarily, but he'd never met Jake nor did he know how they had come to settle in Winston.

When at last the receptionist paged to remind him of a luncheon appointment, Ira asked. "Will you take our case, sir?"

"Even if I have to pay you!" he said enthusiastically. "I may never again have the opportunity to defend a moonshine runner who goes on to become a Grand Ole Opry Star. Call me if you have further questions or information," he added. "If I don't hear from you, have Mary Sue and J.D. here in my office at nine o'clock April 22."

When Jake dropped Ira off at home later that evening there was a message from the sheriff. "Howard brought this by earlier today," Mary Ellen told him. "He said he didn't know what it was about, but Baxter said it was important."

Ira opened the envelope and read. "Come to my office in the morning,"

"That was short and sweet," he said as he handed the message to Mary Ellen.

"Have any idea what it's about?" she asked.

"No, but you can bet it can't be good."

When Ira walked into Baxter's office the next morning he knew immediately he was right. On the corner of his desk lay a Carolina newspaper. On the front page was an article with headlines that read, **Virginia Teenager Arrested For Running Moonshine.** He didn't bother to read the article; he knew all too well what it contained. He did notice the paper was a few days old. Baxter quickly folded it and stuffed it into a drawer.

"What do you think we ought do about this?"

"Do you still believe my girl had something to do with hauling shine?"

"Not for me to say."

"Then it's your call, I figure. Anyone else know about the article?"

"Not yet, but it won't remain a secret forever. I spoke to the sheriff down in Surry County and he says there's nothing he can do. He was the one who mailed me this copy of the newspaper. Go on back to the farm and let me think about this some more, I'll let you know something in a day or so."

Ira sat on the front porch as the evening sun slowly disappeared. He was watching the new farm hand Baxter had hired to replace John Robert. He was tossing forks of hay from the top of a stack near the edge of a meadow across the fence onto the pasture. A large herd of prime beef cattle came rushing to eat their fill before bedding down for the night. An entire week went by with no word from Baxter, and Ira had never felt so helpless.

Mid winter was lashing out with a fury, and he felt as trapped as a caged animal. The wind blew so hard it seemed the snow was coming horizontally. His cruiser had sat idle for days and was now buried beneath a large white mound. He spent his days helping with the livestock and most of the nights walking the floor or sitting in front of the living room window staring down over the snow-covered fields. Drifts piled higher against the split-rail fences with each passing day. Almost no traffic moved on the snow-covered road, and it seemed as if the whole world was coming to a standstill.

The sheriff's farm had become very profitable in recent years, thanks to the efforts put forth by the Duncan family. Ira reflected on the scorching hot days of summer he had toiled in the fields to make them produce, the bitter cold winter days he had spent hours feeding and tending the livestock. He recalled the times the twins brought newborn calves inside to be bottle fed for fear they would not survive.

Ira pulled his wool-lined jump jacket tighter around him to ward off the chilling wind blowing across the northern peaks of the mountain. But, it was not the weather causing the cold chills running up and down his spine. It was what might befall his family as a result of Baxter's actions. He just hoped the sheriff would remember the Duncan family's loyalty before he made his decision.

Chapter Ten

A HASTY DECISION

On the following Monday morning, Ira's hopes were totally destroyed. He was about to begin helping with the livestock feeding when the red bubble atop Baxter's cruiser came into view. It was the only part of the car that could be seen above the windblown snowdrifts beside the road. As soon as the cruiser stopped at the end of the lane and Deputy Barton got out to open the gate, Ira knew the news was not going to be good. The sheriff came racing up the lane, plowing through the snowdrifts. A broken tire chair banged the rear fender sending large clumps of ice flying in all directions. Baxter motioned for Ira to get in while Barton cleared snow from the parked cruiser. He reached him a copy of the county newspaper without saying a word. The heavy black type on the front page said it all: **Local Couple Facing Felony Charges.** Baxter waited in silence while Ira read the article in its entirety. The paper was very accurate in describing details of the arrests. Complete details of the arrests were in print, including J.D.'s name and the description of the automobile. The only detail not mentioned was Mary Sue's name only because she was a minor.

Ira folded the paper turned to the sheriff. "What now?" he asked.

"I am forced to relieve you of your duties Ira, The county can ill afford to employ a member of law enforcement whose family indulges in running moonshine, to say nothing of the embarrassment this will bring to my office. I'll need your badge, gun, uniforms, and any other items belonging to the county. You do understand, of course."

"I fully understand," was Ira's rapid response. "It's clear you're more concerned about your embarrassment than you are at getting to the truth. You know full well my daughter had nothing to do with hauling illegal whiskey. The least you could do is give us a chance to defend against these charges before you take such unwarranted action."

Ira was finding it hard to control his anger, but he didn't care. He was far more interested in protecting Mary Sue's reputation than preventing undue embarrassment to Baxter or the Sheriff's Office. "I guess I'm back to being your tenant farmer, right?"

Baxter lowered his head and mumbled in a low seemingly apologetic voice. "I got to let you go, Ira."

"You mean move from the farm?"

Baxter nodded.

Ira sat for a moment in a state of absolute disbelief. "How long before we have to move?" were the only words he could manage?

"Sixty days should be enough, don't you think?"

Ira had no response. He got out of the car and started for the house.

"Check the oil, Barton," Baxter commanded.

The deputy raised the hood on Ira's squad car and was knocked off his feet. An explosion under the hood sent billows of smoke into the air. Ira rushed to Barton's aid and helped him to his feet. It was merely a smoke bomb and the deputy was unharmed but whoever planted it had surely gotten their message across.

"Thanks, Ira, you're getting a raw deal. If there's anything I can do, just let me know. He won't get away with this; it will cost him somewhere down the road. He offered me your position as chief deputy, but I declined."

Ira rushed inside, gathered the items that belonged to the sheriff's department, and was back before the smoke cleared. He opened the rear door of Baxter's cruiser and tossed the bundle onto the back seat. He watched as the county vehicles disappeared behind the snowdrifts before going back inside to break the news to the family.

When Mary Sue came home, she brought all her school supplies with her. She tossed them on the floor in the middle of the living room floor and promised she would never go back to school again. The students had changed from treating her as a celebrity to that of a convict in a matter of days.

For three weeks he did nothing but worry, waiting for the storm to let up. Watching the windblown snow being driven across the fields was driving him crazy. He'd had no means of transportation since John Robert left for the coast; but up until now, he hadn't needed any. He had taken care of any personal business while on duty, with the sheriff's permission; but now, he was becoming desperate.

Near the end of the month, he made up his mind he would wait no longer. Time was running out, and he decided he would rather die than to ask Baxter for an extension. Their food supply, with the exception of what they grew, was almost depleted. He determined that whatever he did would be better than doing nothing.

Ira had less than thirty dollars to his name and pride made him refuse one penny from his daughter. He got up before dawn each morning, walked a mile and a half to the main highway and hitched a ride into town. Most days he could get a ride back to the farm by nightfall; if not he slept on a bench in the N & W depot. He repeated this process day after day for almost a month with no success.

On a bitter cold Friday shortly before dusk, he began walking toward home feeling totally defeated. He was so lost in thoughts of desperation he was unaware that a vehicle was being driven along beside him. The loud blast of a horn brought him back to reality. It was Deputy Barton gesturing for him to get in.

Ira's half-frozen hand fumbled with the door handle. When he was finally able to get inside, he was so cold he could hardly speak. That didn't matter all he really had to do was listen. Howard knew about his situation and was so excited to be the bearer of good news he could hardly wait to tell his friend and former colleague.

"I have found a place for you and your family, Ira," he began. "It's not much and it's not real easy to get to, but the rent is cheap. It's located beside the railroad tracks on the banks of the Clinch River in the southern end of the county."

Ira made a weak attempt at a smile and started to say something, but Howard cut him off. "There's more, I have also got the guarantee of a job if you're interested. It's in a coal mine near Kimball, West Virginia. The work is hard, but the pay is pretty good."

Ira sat for a full minute unable to speak, but it had nothing to do with the weather. The car heater was warming his body but the news was doing a far greater job warming his heart. Again he started to say something but like before Howard kept talking. "I'll need to let the people know before the end of the weekend."

"I'll take it," Ira managed.

"The house or the job?"

"Both. Thanks Howard. Do you think the sheriff would mind if you take me home?"

"Sure he would, but I'm off duty. Let's go."

Howard parked the cruiser in front of Baxter's farmhouse, and Ira insisted he come inside. He summoned all the family to the living room and asked the deputy to give them the news.

Howard began by telling them the house was a large one story about one mile from Cleveland near the banks of the Clinch River. The railroad tracks lay between the house and one of the finest fishing holes in the Clinch. "The only access to the house is by way of a narrow road that runs along side the railroad tracks. This means the children will have to change schools and walk to

Cleveland to catch the school bus. There is ample area for a large garden but little else, which means there will be lots of time for fishing. Not the ideal location, but it is the best I could do. I realize what you must have being going through and I wanted to get you out of Baxter's clutches. By the way, he's getting quite a reputation as being a womanizer and is rapidly losing popularity."

"Tell'em about the job," Ira coaxed.

"It's inside a coal mine up in the hills of West Virginia, between Kimball and Keystone, I'm told. The shifts are long, the work is hard, but the pay is good. Two or three fellows in Cleveland work in that mine and, they travel together. They leave early each Sunday afternoon and get back home late Friday night."

The room was filled with mixed emotions. Mary Ellen was so happy to see the relief on Ira's face, she was ready to begin packing immediately. She had heard stories about gambling, drinking, and association with the female tenants in the Keystone boarding houses, but she completely trusted her husband. Anyway, she felt these circumstances would change right away.

The twins were excited about living within a mile of town, not to mention being able to fish anytime they wanted. The walk to catch a school bus meant nothing, they sometimes walked further than that to school already.

Mary Sue decided she didn't care where she lived. She didn't plan to go to school in Cleveland or anywhere else until after the trial. She would keep practicing her singing, record her best numbers, and contact the recording studio. If she were convicted she would forget about becoming an attorney and pursue a career in the field of entertainment. If she were exonerated, she would go back to high school, on to college and then law school.

Granny had a much different outlook. She was going to miss her weekly visit to her ladies club She'd watched Ira grow from childhood into manhood and wasn't as confident as Mary Ellen in his ability to remain faithful. She, like the twins, loved to fish; but she hated the thought of hearing those annoying trains roaring past day and night. And, she was harboring feelings of revenge toward Baxter. She had never liked him, for reasons she rarely made known, and she wanted to see him pay for what he had done.

Howard stayed far into the night and came early the next morning to take Ira and Mary Ellen to Cleveland. He took them to inspect the home he'd found and introduced them to one of the miners who worked in Kimball.

A week later the Duncans were living on the Clinch, and Ira was working inside a coal mine in West Virginia.

CHAPTER ELEVEN

LIFE ON THE RIVER

The brutal days of winter gave way to spring, and the Duncan family was making every effort to adjust. Living along the banks of the big river, as the twins called it, was quite a contrast to that of farm living.

The boys accepted the change much better than the other members of the family. Seems they never had an idle minute. They changed schools with very little difficulty and, right away, began making new friends. They actually looked forward to the walk along the tracks into Cleveland to catch the school bus each morning. They took turns tossing pebbles at frogs, turtles, ducks, or didapper or any other creature that stuck its head out of the water. The object was not to hurt any of the wildlife, but to see who could come the closest without actually harming them.

Just beyond the N & W tracks and across the Clinch was the main highway leading into the south end of Cleveland. The house where the Duncan family lived was at almost the same elevation as the highway so they were able to see everything coming into or leaving town.

Occasionally the twins made a game of waiting until the bus came into view and then racing along the tracks in order to be at their stop before it crossed the river. Granny also watched the traffic traveling along the highway. She almost never saw anyone she knew unless it was one of the regular fisherman with whom she had become acquainted. One vehicle she did recognize, however, was that of the Sheriff. He had gotten word that Deputy Barton was making regular visits to the Duncan family, and he was making sure he did not do so while he was on duty.

Mary Sue, unlike the twins, refused to change schools. She'd endured enough embarrassment from people she knew and was not about to subject herself to being ridiculed by strangers. She also postponed her phone call to the recording studio in Nashville. Instead she got a job in a clothing store in the middle of town. She walked the tracks to work with the twins when she could but was rarely off from work when they came home in the afternoons. She worked as many hours as the proprietor would allow then came home to relax by listening to her favorite radio station. She memorized almost every top country hit and practiced them over and over.

Often times she would stand on the back porch facing the river. She'd turn on her tape recorder and lay the mike on a chair near the open door. The porch was her stage and the whole world was her audience. If someday she had the opportunity to become a recording artist, she would be ready; but that was not her ambition. Her goal was to earn enough money to pay her attorney fees, clear her name, and move to Winston where no one knew her.

Mary Ellen became totally withdrawn and spent much of the time alone. She planted flowers in every corner of the yard, picked strawberries along the tracks, worked in the vegetable garden, or whatever she could do to pass the time. She'd spend hours baking gingerbread cakes, molasses cookies, or anything else she could think of to remind Ira of home. She'd pack large quantities of these goodies in a feed sack pillowcase for him to take to the boarding house. She always stashed a note somewhere among these items telling him how much she missed him. And, rain or shine, she walked the track with him every Sunday afternoon to meet his ride back to Kimball.

The miners traveled in a large black nine passenger Dodge Power Wagon that reminded Mary Ellen of a hearse. She and Ira would sit on a bench in front of the local hardware store waiting for the wagon to arrive. They'd share a RC Cola and dream of the time when he would no longer have to work the mines.

Mary Ellen would watch until the wagon was completely out of sight before walking the tracks back home. It was while making these trips she dwelt on the things that disturbed her most. She thought about the possibility of an automobile wreck during the long trip back to West Virginia or the horrible mining accidents she often heard about. And try as she might, she could not erase the thoughts of the pretty women working at or living in the boarding houses. These were the times she despised most, and the times her hatred for Baxter grew stronger. Just to recall the few occasions, she had gone out with him while she was single made her angry.

Granny was the most outspoken about her feelings. She was aware of Mary Ellen's feeling of loneliness and respected her desire to be alone. She did, however, come in contact with others who were willing to listen as she vented her frustrations. She became friends with a widow lady named Gertie about her own age who lived about half-mile further down the tracks. She and her new friend spent many hours together fishing along the banks of the Clinch and each one would fish by herself if the other had business elsewhere.

The deep, smooth-running waters beside where they lived were as Deputy Barton had described. It was one of the best known fishing holes for miles around, and it attracted sportsmen from far and near. It was here Granny found folks more than willing to listen to her crucify Baxter. Several of the local fishermen shared her feelings because the sheriff's reputation was becoming widely known. Many times the stories were so interesting, simply yelling at each other across the water passed them on.

The letters from Ida Mae became more frequent. Both she and Jake were in total shock at the news Baxter had ordered them off the farm. She explained Jake had not come to visit because he felt partially to blame for all that had taken place. Neither had he been back to the mountain to help with his daddy's logging business. He had, she emphasized, made several trips to the attorney Wallace's office in Mt. Airy, in preparation of Mary Sue's defense. She promised she and Jake would come get her the day before the trial.

Ida Mae insisted her daddy not take time off from work for fear he might get fired. "Please make him know that Jake is doing everything that can be done to insure Mary Sue's defense," she begged. "And, tell Mother that Daddy needs her at home much more than we do here in North Carolina. The trial may go on for two or three days and she is under enough stress already. I have Howard Barton's home telephone number, and he's promised he will help us keep you informed. The deputy knows full well Baxter gave Daddy a raw deal, and he will do anything to help him get even."

Howard was indeed a close friend. He and Ira had grown up on the same side of the mountain. They'd attended the same school, shared the same swimming holes and spent hours in the woods hunting game for food or herbs to be sold in the fall. They'd worked side by side on neighboring farms, while growing up, for a few cents per day. Ira was proud when he was hired as chief deputy to be working with someone as trustworthy as his long time friend.

Howard never ceased being a friend to the Duncans even through the troubled times they endured. He came to Cleveland at least twice a week to make sure they were okay. If he were in a rush, he'd check with Mary Sue at the clothing store; if not, he'd drive along the tracks until he found Granny somewhere on the banks of the river. He always traveled in his private vehicle so the sheriff would not have reason to reprimand him.

Granny trusted Howard and found it easy to tell him exactly what was on her mind. She told him how she had neither liked or trusted Baxter and how she could not wait for the day he would pay for what he had done to her family. Little did she know that her opportunity to seek revenge was close at hand.

It happened during mid-afternoon on the very day Mary Sue was in Mt Airy to face the judge. Baxter was cruising along the Clinch hoping to chance upon anyone who might have heard some results of the trial. He saw Granny on the riverbank some good distance away from the house, and he could see Mary Ellen sitting on the back porch with her head in her hands. He knew John Robert was no longer at home and was relatively certain the twins were in school. Ira was in West Virginia deep inside a coal mine so he was not about to let an opportunity like this pass.

He drove slowly along the tracks paying attention to anything that moved. He parked the cruiser and was walking toward the back porch before Mary Ellen knew he was on the place. When she saw him, she was scared out of her mind. She knew he had to be bringing bad news. A thousand thoughts flooded her mind, the worst had happened in North Carolina or there had been a tragic mining accident.

"What's happened?' she asked in a voice that was somewhere near panic.

"Nothing, nothing at all, I just dropped by to say hello."

The sound of a male voice aroused Granny who was dozing just inside. Worrying about Ira and the outcome of the trial had kept her awake most of the night so she was taking this time to catch forty winks. She was so tired, in fact, she declined a day's fishing with her friend Gertie. She immediately became aware of whose voice it was so she did not move.

"Just making sure you were alright," was Baxter's next comment.

Granny was nobody's fool. She knew exactly why he was there and it was not because he was concerned about Mary Ellen's health. Just as she thought about using some non-Christian like adjectives to tell him what kind of a person he was, she noticed Mary Sue's tape recorder. She was lucky to be in a position so as to be seen by Mary Ellen and yet be hidden from the sheriff. At the first opportunity she pointed her finger downward, pointing at the button that turned on the recorder. Mary Ellen knew exactly what she was doing so she played her role to the hilt.

"I'm fine I guess, William; but it's nothing like living on the farm."

"I'm really sorry things turned out as they did, Mary Ellen; but I was left with no choice. You do understand?"

"I guess," she replied.

"I bet you get lonely, being here by yourself most of the time, I mean."

Mary Ellen shrugged her shoulders.

"How does it look for your daughter? The trial and all."

"It looks like she is going to get off scot-free. She is innocent, you know."

"I always figured she was," Baxter agreed.

"Then why did you fire my husband and place our family in an out-of–the-way
place like this?" she questioned.

"Because, if in fact she was guilty, it would look really bad on the department, you understand."

Mary Ellen had heard the phrase **you understand** so many times it was ringing in her ears.

"So what's going to happen when she's exonerated?"

"Well, it might just be things could go back as they were before Mary Sue got herself into trouble."

"You mean move back onto your farm?"

"That is not beyond the realm of possibility, if . . . ?"

"If what?"

Baxter shuffled his feet, rattled the keys in his pocket, and hesitated for a long moment. "I never did understand why you and Ira got married so soon after you and I quit seeing each other. I was really surprised. You would never even allow me to kiss you goodnight; then before I knew what was happening, you were married and starting a family."

"That's because Ira always treated me like a lady."

"If I had another chance, I would treat you like a lady."

"You mean come visit when there was no one else around?"

"I always knew you were a smart girl, Mary Ellen," he said as he took a step closer.

Mary Ellen was so angry she could have pushed him from the porch and into the river, but she managed to keep her cool. "If I agree to let you come by when I'm home by myself, are you telling me you would let us move back to the farm?"

"I'd even help you start packing. What do you say?"

"That's blackmail, William! You're supposed to be an officer of the law."

"Sure it is, but you do what ever is necessary to accomplish your goals, you understand."

Granny had heard all she could take. She stepped onto the porch and looked Baxter straight into his eyes. "I'd say you are the scum of the earth. **You understand?**"

Baxter turned the color of buttermilk. "I thought you were fishing." He rushed to his car and slammed the door. "Just let me know if you or the family ever need anything," he yelled, and drove off as if nothing had ever been said.

Granny took Mary Ellen in both arms and squeezed her with all her strength. "I am so sorry for all the bad thoughts; and for the way I've treated you all these years. Please forgive me," she begged. They stood in silence for some time as tears streamed down their faces.

When at last Granny regained her composure, she stepped back inside. "I don't know anything about all these new gadgets, but see if I recorded anything that idiot said."

Mary Ellen had watched Mary Sue so often she knew exactly how to operate the machine. She let the tape rewind, pressed the play button and both ladies held their breath. The reels started turning and for a moment there was not a sound. Then Baxter's voice came on loud and clear, "Just making sure you were alright."

"Granny, you're a genius. I'm so happy I don't know if I should laugh or cry. I'll love you forever."

Granny was every bit as pleased and excited as her daughter-in-law. It was the first time anyone had ever used the word *genius* to describe her, and it was also the first time Mary Ellen had shown her so much affection.

"Let's you and me laugh, and we'll let Old Baxter do the crying."

The ladies carefully removed the tape and stored it in a safe place. "Just wait until I tell Ira," Mary Ellen said.

"We better give this a lot of consideration before we tell Ira or do anything," Granny suggested.

"Why do we need to wait?"

"Because Ira will kill him; isn't that reason enough?"

"You're right; and if you hadn't been here, I would have tried to kill him myself, but we have to do something."

The ladies were quiet and in deep thought for several minutes.

"Howard! That's our answer." Granny exclaimed. "We can trust him, and he'll know exactly what we should do. He will be by tomorrow with news about Mary Sue's trial, and we can tell him then. We have to be very careful not to let the twins or anyone else know what happened here today."

* * * * *

The atmosphere in the Duncan home was the best it had ever been. Granny was up before dawn and Mary Ellen was overwhelmed to awake to the smell of coffee. Not a word was spoken about the change in Granny's attitude, but Mary Ellen knew it was a small gesture of apology.

The twins were off to school, and the ladies sat on the porch awaiting Deputy Barton's arrival. It was difficult to determine which was most pressing, finding out the results of Mary Sue's trial or telling Barton about Baxter's visit. They were so anxious for him to hear what the sheriff had done they had already placed the reel on the recorder. It didn't take long for them to decide which matter would be taken care of first. Shortly before noon, they could see the deputy making his earliest arrival.

"Good morning, ladies. A little while ago I received news from North Carolina. I promised to let you know at once, but the only news I have is really no news. They have decided to have a bench trial; and it has been postponed until next Monday. Their attorney is not as hopeful as to the outcome as he was earlier, and Mary Sue is becoming really depressed. It might be helpful if you and Ira could go down for the weekend. If you decide to do so, you are welcome to use my vehicle."

"That's a wonderful idea, Mary Ellen. The twins and I will stay home and fish all weekend. Now, tell Howard about our news."

"What news? Is Ira okay?" he questioned.

"Oh, he's fine, but you must promise that what we're about to tell you will remain a secret. Not even Ira can know until you have helped us decide what we should do."

"It must be something really important if you don't want Ira to know."

"We think it is," Granny said, "but we'll let you decide."

"I give my word; now what's this all about?"

The ladies began relaying the happenings of the day before. Howard stood so astounded at what he was hearing he was utterly speechless. He listened intently to every word as the almost unbelievable episode unfolded.

As her story ended Mary Ellen asked Granny to turn on the recorder. As the deputy listened the expression on his face relayed what he was thinking. Excitedly he said, "At last you ladies are going to be able to help me and Ira see that Baxter gets just what he deserves. You better believe I'll help you, but you'll have to trust me. I'll need to make a copy of the tape, and it will take a few days to do what must be done."

Chapter Twelve

RETURN TO MT. AIRY

The morning of April 22 was one of the most fearful times Mary Sue had known in all her seventeen years. She, Ida Mae and Jake were sitting in the outer office of the law firm of Smith, Donnelly and Wallace. Jake kept reassuring her things were never as bad as they seemed. She fully intended to pass the word along to her knees if they would quit shaking long enough. Ida Mae had made every effort to tell her as gently as possible the severity of her charges. She waited until the last minute to let her know that transporting illegal whiskey across state lines was a federal offense and might result in severe punishment.

They also told her that because she was minor and had never been in trouble before, they felt the judge would show her leniency. "A lot depends on J.D. and his attorney. If he is willing to say you had no knowledge of the crime and can convince the court he is telling the truth, all your charges may be dismissed. If, on the other hand, he tries to place equal blame on you in order to get a lighter sentence you might both be in trouble."

"And if he does?" Mary Sue asked as the receptionist announced Attorney Wallace was ready to see them.

"Then I'll kill him myself," Jake whispered.

The receptionist ushered them down the hall to William Wallace's office. When she opened the door, Mary Sue was totally amazed. She had never been in a place so elaborately furnished in her life. The carpet on the floor was so thick it felt as if it should be mowed instead of vacuumed. A large portrait of the Honorable William Wallace Sr. hung on the wall directly behind a solid cherry partners desk. Bookcases filled with leather bound books surrounded the portrait. A half-circle of plush chairs encircled the front of the desk. The attorney welcomed them to his office and asked that they be seated. He introduced himself to Mary Sue and stated that he was aware of the aspects of the case.

Mary Sue wondered how anyone could afford an attorney who enjoyed such luxuries. Better to spend life in jail than to have to work all her life to pay for his services, she reasoned.

"Any new developments, Billy?" Jake wanted to know.

Mary Sue shook her head in disbelief; she was amazed to learn her brother-in-law, a redneck from the mountains, would be on first name basis with someone of such high standings.

"Well, it's like this," the attorney began. "Your case was on the court docket to be tried by Judge Wallace. But, since he is my father and he and my brother have become close friends with some of your family members, he found it necessary to remove himself from the case. Another Judge will be appointed; and you, like Jake's brother of course, have the option of having a bench trial or having your case heard by a jury."

"What do you recommend, sir?" Mary Sue spoke for the first time.

"Bench trial," Wallace spoke without hesitation. "If the two of you, meaning you and Mr. Hurd of course, choose a bench trial, a judge will hear your plea, weigh the evidence; and he alone will decide the degree of punishment. If you choose to have your case heard by a jury, anything could happen. If the jury believes you knew nothing about what Mr. Hurd was hauling, you could be completely exonerated. If we were to have a hung jury, meaning no decision could be reached, we could have to go through the entire procedure all over again. And, I must tell you the worse case scenario, you could be found guilty which means we would have to begin the process of appealing the case."

"How, . . . how much will all this cost?" she stammered.

"We'll get to that in a few moments," the attorney continued. "But before you make your decision there's something you need to know. Mr. Hurd, J.D., has asked me to defend him. I have agreed to do so if, and only if, he agrees to tell me the whole truth; you can substantiate what he says and if you have no objections to my defending him. I realize he may not be at the top of your popularity list at this time, but I think it would be better if I could have both of you tried together-if the prosecuting attorney agrees of course."

Mary Sue looked to Jake to Ida Mae and then to the attorney hoping for any sign that would aid in her decision. There was none.

"You do believe I'm innocent, don't you, Mr. Wallace?" she asked.

"I do. Jake and Ida Mae have thoroughly convinced me of that."

"Then it's a bench trial, and I have no objection to you defending J.D."

Jake smiled, and Ida Mae squeezed her hand indicating they thought she had made a wise decision.

"Now, as for the matter of my fee, I require 100 per cent in advance. You do have a dollar with you, don't you Miss Duncan?"

Mary Sue could not believe what she had heard. She opened her clutch purse and, with a trembling hand, proudly presented the attorney one of her crisp one hundred dollar bills. "I won this down in Winston," she mumbled.

"I heard, and you rightfully deserved it I understand; but we keep no cash here in the office so I'm afraid I have no change"

Jake slipped a dollar bill into her hand, and she in turn gave it to the attorney.

"Would you like a receipt?" he asked.

"That's not at all necessary, sir," she smiled.

"My fees are strictly confidential you understand. J.D. is waiting in another office for my decision to defend him. I'll have my receptionist show him in, and I rather doubt his fee will be as modest."

A moment later J.D. stepped into the office. His expression was that of total embarrassment. If Mary Sue's stare had been a dagger, he would have immediately dropped to the floor. He walked to where she was seated. "I am truly sorry I got you involved in all this," he told her.

Mary Sue did not speak.

"Does that mean you are going to plead guilty?" Wallace asked.

"It does, if you agree to defend me."

"That didn't take long. I'll have to make a few phone calls so why don't you folks go to lunch, and I'll see you back here in my office-say four o'clock?"

J.D. was the first to leave the office. The others followed close behind. "I'll tell him where else he can go as soon as we get outside," Mary Sue informed them.

Ida Mae gently took her by the arm and led her to one side. "Look, Sis, he got you into this mess; and right now, he is the only one who can get you out. So, be nice, ok?"

"I will, I'll even be one of his pallbearers," she snapped.

"No! You have to calm down and think what you're doing. At least be polite until this is over, and then I'll help you kill him."

Mary Sue knew she was not serious but still she appreciated her sister's concern. She took a few deep breaths and agreed to do her best. They joined Jake, J.D. and Mr. Hurd who had been waiting outside all the while.

"I know of a little diner near the edge of town, so let's all go eat" Jake suggested as they approached Ida Mae's car. "I'll drive."

Mary Sue was anything but fond of the idea, but she offered no objections. Neither she nor anyone else spoke a word during the twenty-minute ride. When they entered the diner she took the seat as far away from J.D. as was possible and still be at the same table. Still no one talked except to give the waitress his or her order for drinks. When at last it seemed the silence was deafening J.D. began to speak.

"I'm offering no excuses understand, but let me tell you what brought all this about. I never liked the logging business when I grew up at home," he began. "It was back-breaking labor for man and beast day after day from dawn till dusk, not to mention the danger. Someone was getting injured almost weekly. You can easily see what it's done to Daddy," he continued, pointing to Mr. Hurd's crippled body. "So I decided I wanted to be like Jake. I wanted to leave the mountains, go to a big city, where I could earn twice the money doing half the work. And, like you Jake, I wanted to master the art of shooting pool. So, at the first opportunity I did just that. I started hitchhiking north and three days later, I found myself in Detroit, Michigan."

"I thought you told me you were from Chicago," Mary Sue interrupted.

"I lied," he confessed. "Anyway I landed a job in a GM plant and I lived for almost five years in Detroit. I earned much more than twice the money I expected, but I never mastered the art of saving nor did I master the art of shooting pool, although I tried. I spent the days working, and the nights at the bars and the pool tables. By the end of most weekends, I was broke so on Monday morning I began the process all over again.

Then a few months ago, I met a fellow from North Carolina. He came to Detroit for only one purpose. He wanted to earn enough money as quickly as possible so he could purchase a new car and get into the racing business. All he talked about was how auto racing was going to become the fastest growing sport in this country.

Before I knew it I had given up the idea of becoming a pool shark and devoted all my interest in also becoming a race car driver. I bought my new Dodge, with almost no down payment, took a two-week vacation, and headed to North Carolina. Those boys down there know how to build race cars you know."

"You told me you paid cash for your car; I guess that was also a lie." Mary Sue let him have it again.

J.D. only nodded, "I guess I just wanted to impress you."

"You've sure made an impression alright," she snapped.

Ida Mae gave her a gentle kick under the table. "Go on, J.D.," she said.

"I had those fellows do everything that could be done to make my Dodge run faster. Then two weeks after I went back to work, I got laid off. Things were getting bad in and around Detroit so I headed back to the mountains. I told no one but Daddy, and I asked him to help so I wouldn't lose the Dodge.

The logging business was at a virtual standstill, so hauling whiskey seemed the only other way. I promise; Mom, Jake, nor anyone else knew anything about this. What can I do to make up for what I've done?" he asked Mary Sue.

"You can tell it to the judge!" she snapped again. "But you know, that Dodge really is a pretty car J.D.," she added in a much more civil tone.

For the first time she brought smiles to everyone at the table.

They finished their meal, sipped drinks at the diner for an hour or so and then returned to the law office. It was four o'clock on the dot, and the attorney was waiting for them.

"I have talked to the prosecuting attorney. He is fair but he is very hard-nosed and will soon be running for re-election. He will not reduce the charges but he has agreed not to object to minimum sentencing. Since you have agreed to a bench trial, another judge will hear your case next Monday morning. He and my father are friends and Daddy will surely discuss the circumstances leading up to the offense. And he will not neglect to tell him of the kindness Jake and Ida Mae have shown to our family.

They are both well-respected Officers of the Court and want to see justice done, but they can also be very understanding. You must tell the truth J.D. You must plead guilty and throw yourself on the mercy of the court. I can't promise anything, but that is the best I can do."

* * * * *

They left the attorney's office and headed to Chestnut Street. It was only four days until time for the trial, so it was useless to make another trip back to Virginia.

For the first time in months there were no guest in Jake and Ida Mae's home so there was lodging space for the members of both families. And, since J.D. had agreed to take full responsibility for the crime, tensions had begun to ease. They had the whole weekend to enjoy the sights of the city and they intended to take full advantage of the opportunity.

The men folk spent the first couple of days doing their own thing while Ida Mae and her little sister did almost nothing but shop. Mary Sue still had all of her five hundred dollars prize money; and since she had no attorney fees, she saw no reason to carry all of it back to the mountain. She bought a new dress for herself, one for her mother, and one for Granny. She purchased a new suit for Ira, a new hat for Mr. Hurd, and new fishing gear for the twins. She also bought a large "Welcome Friends" doormat for the front porch of Jake and Ida Mae's home.

J.D. would not hear of her spending money on him, but he did persuade her to promise she would come at least once with Jake to visit him in prison. It was getting late and being Friday night most of the laborers were off from work and were already on the streets in search of some fun and excitement so Jake, Ida Mae and their families headed for home. As they turned onto Chestnut Street, they saw a vehicle parked in front of their house. It was Deputy Howard's automobile, and in It, sat Ira and Mary Ellen who had come to spend the weekend.

It was a beautiful lazy early spring Saturday morning in the city of Winston. The sun was just beginning to emerge from beneath a sea of darkness to welcome the dawning of a new day. Framed only by ocean-blue sky it cast its rays on lingering dewdrops clinging to the maple trees that lined either side of Chestnut Street. The sounds of an awakening city occasionally rang out and then faded.

Robins chirped as they hopped about on the tender new grass meticulously choosing just the right material needed for nesting. Grey squirrels ran from place to place scavenging for anything suitable for an early morning meal.

Ira and Mr. Hurd, both early risers, sat on the porch of Jake and Ida Mae's aging southern plantation home talking of the days gone by. Having grown up in the same era, in the same area, and being almost exactly the same age only added to their discussion. Neither cast blame on the other's family because of past wrongdoings. Having grown up in the mountains during extremely hard times, they could appreciate the need for participating in slightly unlawful endeavors on rare occasions. Both had children who had at one time barely escaped the wrath of the law.

Ira, although in law enforcement, did not place himself outside the realm of understanding the necessity to survive. It was not his goal to bring suffering on those around him who were still struggling to overcome post war hardships. To sell a jug or so of mountain dew for medicinal purposes was a matter to be overlooked. Many times no money changed hands; it was merely traded for a few frying chickens or a pig needed to feed one's family. It was those who ran large amounts of shine, because of greed instead of need, he felt obligated to help see punished.

It was nearly two hours before another movement was heard inside the dwelling. The younger folks had chosen to sleep in as long as possible. No one had plans for the day except for the surprise outing Jake and Ida Mae had planned for the evening.

Near mid-morning Jake pushed a serving cart onto the porch. On it was a steaming hot pot of coffee and a large pitcher of orange juice. A moment later a local catering service delivered a huge platter of ham biscuits and a box of freshly baked donuts. "I've always wanted to know how the elite folks in the world lived," J.D. said jokingly.

"It did not come because of our labor," Ida Mae was quick to reply. "It was because we befriended a lonely kind-hearted lady named Sarah. In return for a few evenings of caring, she left us a small fortune. Because of being kind to those in need, she had acquired great wealth; and she asked nothing in return except we continue that tradition."

"Then I'm going to start being kind to everybody I know," J.D. replied.

"How about starting right now and bring me another donut," Jake suggested.

They ate, drank, and relaxed for most of the day, and became more acquainted with each other's family. They said nothing of the upcoming challenges facing them the following week. They did, however, constantly urge their hosts to tell them about their evening's entertainment, but they did not succeed. "Just be ready by eight o'clock" was all they could learn. And ready they were.

At seven-thirty, still no one except Jake and Ida Mae knew what was in store. When everyone was dressed, they piled into two vehicles and headed down town. They parked in front of the Wellington Dinner Theater. and were greeted by a doorman who led them inside. Mary Sue watched in amazement as two fellows who were dressed alike drove off in their automobiles. "Where do they think they're going?" she questioned, rather startled.

Ida Mae could not help but smile; a few months earlier she would have been just as bewildered. "They're parking attendants, sweetie; I'll explain later."

A tall good-looking man dressed in a tux and bow tie ushered them to a table near a stage. The curtains were drawn but soft music was coming from behind them. A waiter laid a menu in front of each of them and stood patiently waiting to take their order. Mary Sue was glad her sister was seated next to her because

113

half of what was on the menu she could not pronounce and had never heard of. She waited until everyone else finished ordering and then whispered to Ida Mae in a joking manner, "I'll have a steak, baked tater, rolls and a salad; and you can order in whatever language you like."

They listened to the soft music and ate until no could hold another bite. Then, at exactly nine o'clock the curtain began to rise and the stage came into full view. Mary Sue almost fell from her chair when a young man stepped to the mike. "Good evening ladies and gentlemen, I'm Eddie Mayfield; and I will be your entertainer for the night."

"You guys knew he would be here all along, didn't you?" she asked.

Ida Mae simply squeezed her hand. "We thought you could use a little cheering up," she said.

Eddie burst into one of Hank William's latest hits; and when he finished, he received a well deserved round of applause. He sang another song or two then introduced the members of his band. "And, now let me introduce the newest member of our group, Miss Rebecca Ray."

Eddie and the young lady did a great job. They took turns doing singles and then duets. Mary Sue watched every move and listened to every note. She had to admit she was a little envious to say the least. After an hour and a half into the show, she got the surprise of her life. Eddie stepped to the mike once again and spoke to the audience. "And now ladies and gentlemen it gives me great pleasure to introduce one of the most talented up and coming stars to come along in years. She will be joining Miss Ray and me for the remainder of the evening, so make welcome from the hills of Virginia, Miss Mary Sue Duncan."

Mary Sue was absolutely stunned. She sat motionless for a moment. She had no idea Eddie even knew she was in the state let alone in the building. At last a waiter came to the table to usher her to the stage. "I'll get you for this," she whispered to Ida Mae.

Eddie's band did an intro to "Your Cheating Heart." Eddie sang the first verse and the ladies joined in on the chorus. Before the end of the song the crowd was on their feet. Rebecca gave her a gentle hug and whispered, "You're every bit as good as Eddie said you were; welcome aboard."

This settled the butterflies in her stomach and for the remainder of the evening Mary Sue had the time of her life. She welcomed another opportunity to perform before a live audience; but most of all, she was glad her mother and daddy was there to hear her sing with a professional band. It made all the practicing with her tape recorder on the back porch by the river worthwhile.

When the show ended, Mary Sue brought Eddie and his band down onto the floor to meet her family. She introduced them one at a time and thanked him for one of the most fun-filled evenings of her life.

Eddie introduced Rebecca as his fiancée; and, for a brief moment jealously ran through Mary Sue's veins like an electric current. Then she remembered her dream of becoming a successful attorney and the promise she made to herself that she would first achieve her goal and allow love to come later.

Eddie, the members of his band, and her family visited until closing time. When it was time to leave, Eddie promised Mary Sue she could join his show any time she chose. And, Rebecca promised to send her an engraved invitation to their wedding.

CHAPTER THIRTEEN

THE TRIAL

At last it was Monday morning, the day of reckoning for the "outlaws" from Virginia. Ida Mae, Jake and their families were up before sunrise making preparation for the journey north to Mt. Airy. J.D. and his daddy led the way with Jake, Ida Mae and Mary Sue following close behind. Ira and Mary Ellen had left the morning before for fear that a lost shift of work might cost Ira his job. But they left with the assurance that Deputy Barton would be contacted the minute the judge made his ruling. They also knew that the deputy would in turn get the news to the folks back home.

Mary Sue had full confidence in Attorney Wallace's ability to defend her, but still she did not expect to get off easy. She felt sure she would have to pay an enormous fine.

Suddenly, she was panic-stricken. She was so thrilled at not having to pay an attorney's fee she completely forgot about the possibility of having to pay a fine. Her stomach began to churn as she realized she had only $150 of her prize money left." Great time to be thinking about paying a fine now," she thought, as they turned into the parking lot of the city municipal building. J.D. and his daddy were already waiting for their arrival.

As previously arranged, Attorney Wallace was waiting in the main lobby. The look on his face was anything but a welcome sight. He made a stab at a cordial greeting and quickly escorted them down a wide hallway and into a witness room just outside the courtroom. He placed a brief case on one end of a long conference table and asked them all to be seated. He extracted a manila folder from the case and fumbled through several pages.

"The case is not exactly going as I had planned," he began. "My father's friend, the judge who was scheduled to hear your case, has suddenly taken ill. Another circuit court judge, whom I know nothing about, has been appointed to replace him. I had one of my investigators check him out as quickly as I learned of the change. I must admit I am not overly excited about their findings.

"He's only been on the bench for a short time, appointed due to the death of another judge. My report states he's a few years past the age of retirement, most always irritable, and is accused of rendering extremely harsh punishment. I have submitted a written copy of Mr. Hurd's guilty plea and one of your innocence to the prosecutor and to the judge for review. I think I have convinced the prosecutor to be as gentle as possible; but what the judge does, remains to be seen."

This was the last thing Mary Sue needed to hear, but there was no time for discussion. It was almost time for their case to be heard and to be late was out of the question. She and J.D. followed attorney Wallace into the almost empty courtroom and were seated on either side of him at the defense table. Mary Sue had never been in a courtroom before and just being so close to the bench made her feel intimidated.

"Are we the only people to be tried today?" J.D. wanted to know.

"Oh, no, but because Miss Duncan is a minor, the case will be heard in closed court. Only those who have interest in the case will be allowed in the courtroom."

Mary Sue breathed a sigh of relief; at least she would not be embarrassed in front of a crowd.

They waited nervously until a uniformed officer who had been standing near the front asked everyone to rise. He bellowed something about "hear yea, hear yea," and stated that court was now in session. He proclaimed The Honorable Sidney J. Duff to be the presiding judge, and instructed everyone to be quiet and to be seated.

The judge seated himself, yawned a couple of times, poured a glass of water, and picked up his gavel. "Good morning, Mr. Hager," he said to the prosecuting attorney. "Are you ready to get under way?"

"Ready, Your Honor; and good morning to you, sir."

"And, Good morning to you too Mr.–" he paused and looked down at the folder as Wallace interrupted.

"William Wallace, Jr., attorney for the defense, Your Honor."

The judge scratched his head and looked as if he was trying hard to recall something from memory. "You must be Bill's boy," he said.

"That's correct, sir,"

"I've heard a lot about you, out on the course you know."

"Yes, my father is an avid golfer."

Mary Sue could hardly believe how informal the proceedings were going. She was grateful, however; and it helped to relieve some of the tension.

The judge turned to an elderly lady seated at a small table beside him and asked for the name of the first case.

"The state of North Carolina vs. Mary Sue Duncan and James Douglas Hurd, Your Honor." She answered as she was handing the file to the judge.

He opened the file, remained silent and raised his eyebrows several times as he read. "Un huh, Un huh," he repeated while shaking his head. "Transporting illegal whiskey across state lines is a very serious offense. You two fellers are awfully young to be involved in such outrageous endeavors, how do you plead?"

Attorney Wallace and the two defendants rose to their feet. "If it please the court, we have two separate pleas, Your Honor."

"How can that be? Both your clients were in the same vehicle at the time of the arrest, were they not?"

"Mr. Hurd pleads guilty as charged, Your Honor, and asks only that he be shown mercy from the court. Miss Duncan, on the other hand, is guilty only by means of association. She was simply in the wrong place at the wrong time."

"To hear the circumstances surrounding this case would sure be interesting, to say the least. Please continue, Mr. Wallace."

By this time, Ida Mae, Jake and his daddy were beginning to become somewhat nervous. They were afraid it was going to be impossible for the attorney to convince the old judge Mary Sue was not guilty.

The defense attorney explained in every detail how Mary Sue came to be driving the vehicle in question at the time of their arrest. He told of the hardships J.D.'s family had encountered in recent years and strongly emphasized the fact the J.D had no prior record. He also made every effort to make the judge understand that, even though she was in control of the vehicle, his client was completely unaware of the cargo she was hauling.

"Do the two of you agree with the statements your attorney has made to the court, and do each of you agree to the plea he has entered in your behalf?"

Both Mary Sue and J.D. indicated that they did.

"Do you have anything to add to this case?" the judge asked the arresting officer.

"No sir, Your Honor. You have all the facts of the arrest right there in your folder."

"What about you, Mr. Hager?"

To every one's surprise, the prosecutor offered no further comments.

"According to the statement you gave to the magistrate, you obtained the moonshine in the mountains of Southwest Virginia. "Is that correct, Mr. Hurd?"

"Yah, I mean yes sir," was all J.D. could manage.

"Where in Southwest Virginia?"

"Buchanan County."

"How did you come to know about Buchanan County?' the judge continued.

"That's where I grew up, sir, in a little section we called Combs Ridge."

The resemblance of a smile crossed the judge's lips. "Does Tivis Pruner still live up on top of the ridge?"

J.D. was so shocked he could barely answer. "Why, why, he sure does, Your Honor."

"What about Taze and Maudie Shortridge, they still around?"

"Taze is still there, sir; but Miss Maudie, she passed on some years back."

"Old Taze is got to be pushing ninety," the judge continued.

"Ninety-three, last Fourth of July; everybody on the ridge knows when Taze's birthday is."

"Is he still in the same business?"

"Just supervises, Your Honor; the boys have taken over."

The prosecutor sat in total disbelief. He leaned back in his chair, placed his thumbs under his belt and began shaking his head.

The judge suddenly realized he was in court. He cleared his throat and looked down at Hager. "You wanted to say something?"

"Who, me? Oh, no, sir, I was just listening to the updates on the Shortridge family."

The judge squinted his eyes and glared straight at the prosecutor.

Hager immediately got the message. "I mean, no sir; I didn't need to say anything."

"Then I'll get on with this case. After due consideration and having heard from the defendants and their attorney, I am dismissing all charges against Miss Mary Sue Duncan. As for you Mr. Hurd, in as much as you have admitted guilt I must sentence you to three years in the North Carolina State prison. However, since you come from one of the most law-abiding sections of our country, and I'm sure you have learned your lesson, the sentence is suspended. All except for time served, of course. As for your automobile, you'll have to pay one hundred dollars before the sheriff will release it from the pound. Court dismissed."

The attorney thanked the judge and turned to catch up with his clients as they exited the courtroom.

"By the way Mr. Hurd," the judge called after them, "tell Uncle Taze I will be back up to see him at the very first opportunity."

CHAPTER FOURTEEN

THE STORM

Ida Mae and Mary Sue could hardly wait to get to the phone booth outside the courthouse in order to get the news back to Deputy Barton. They knew he would in turn inform their mother and the news would help to relieve some of the stress she was under. Ida Mae dialed the number to the deputy's phone and deposited the forty-five cents the operator requested. Almost instantly she heard a busy signal, and her coins dropped into the return cup. J.D also tried to get news of his good fortune back to the mountain, but his attempts were the same as Ida Mae's. They took turns dialing several more times during the next thirty minutes but to no avail; the lines were continuously busy.

"Let's get started and we'll try again along the way." Ida Mae suggested.

"We?" Mary Sue asked.

"Another surprise, ah Sis, I'm going home with you to spend a few days. Jake has a couple of things to take care down in Winston then he'll come get me in a week or so. Mr. Hurd said I could ride with him and J.D. wants you to ride the Green Dragon, if you'll drive, of course."

"Is that correct, J.D.?"

"I'd be pleased if you would, Mary Sue."

"Then let's go get the Dragon; and if I'm caught hauling anything in the trunk this time, it'll be you."

Jake left for Winston and the others picked up the Dodge and headed north to the mountains. Ida Mae enjoyed the time alone with her father-in-law. It was the first time just the two of them had had an opportunity like this to visit. And Mary Sue was having the time of her life following close behind driving the Green Dragon. She, too, was enjoying getting to know J.D. better. She really believed he only hauled the moonshine in order not to lose his car. As a matter of fact, she sort of felt sorry for him, losing his job and all. She listened as he told how he loved the mountains but hated the logging business and how he wanted to move to the Carolinas and become a race car driver. She loved it when he encouraged her to fall behind Ida Mae and his dad just so she would have to drive faster to catch up. "Maybe you should get into racing, too," he teased.

"No, thank you, I prefer being an attorney. I understand they make a ton of money."

"Boy, you sure got that right," he said without hesitation.

They had been driving up the mountain for a while when it started to rain. Fog was beginning to form; and the further they drove, the thicker it became. Sometimes it was so dense they could barely see the vehicle in front of them. Suddenly, there was an earth-shattering flash of lightning. An almost deafening sound of thunder followed, and it was as if the Heavens opened up. They were in the middle of a down-pour and the fog was as thick as pea soup. Mary Sue had never been so frightened in all her life. She was so nervous it was all she could do not to wet her pants. Her knees began to tremble and the Dodge began to jerk. A large stream of water flowed down the side of the road; and occasionally, stones as large as softballs washed from driveways onto the highway.

"Let me take over," J.D. said as he scooted so close to her she was tightly wedged between him and the driver's door. Her body did not stop trembling but at least she was not in control.

"Where are we?" she asked

"I have no idea; but as long as we've been climbing this mountain, we have to be nearing the top. I hope Daddy remembers there's a little restaurant up ahead and that he has decided to pull off there."

The words were scarcely out of his mouth when a dimly lit neon sign came into view. It said "Mama's Home Cooking Come On In". J.D. wheeled the Dodge into the parking area and barely missed the rear bumper of his daddy's pickup truck. He turned off the ignition and slumped back onto the seat. For the first time Mary Sue realized he was as frightened as she.

They sat for nearly half-hour listening to the rain pound the top of the car. When at last it seemed it was not going to let up, they decided to make a mad dash for the restaurant door with Ida Mae and Mr. Hurd close behind.

They stood dripping for a moment, as the lights inside began to flicker. A middle-aged lady greeted them and handed them two large thirsty towels. "Come in," she said "and sit anywhere you like. As you can see, we're not really busy at the moment."

It didn't take but an instant to know the lady was right. The only other person in the building was a waitress who was seated at one end of the bar. Her elbows were firmly planted on the counter and her chin rested in her hands.

"I'm Magdalene, but most folks just call me Mama" the lady continued. "I'm the proprietor of this overcrowded establishment and this is Irene. She is a pretty good waitress when she's awake."

They took seats at the nearest table as Mama handed a menu to each of them. "What'll you folks have to drink, Coca Cola, ice tea, or coffee?"

"I'll have a strong coffee and cokes for the others," Mr. Hurd told her.

"One in a cup and three in a bottle," She yelled. "Oh, excuse me; Irene is a little hard of hearing."

The waitress who appeared to be somewhat older than Mama jumped to her feet as quickly as if a bolt of lightning had hit her.

"How long has it been raining?" Ida Mae asked.

"Two days, almost non-stop." Mama said as the lights flickered again. "The special for the day is beef stew if you like."

They all agreed stew would be fine, and J.D. asked if they might use her phone.

"I wish you could, but it's been out of order since the storm began. But I guess I shouldn't complain. Our customers tell us that tell us that north of here the storm is the worst they have ever seen. Power is out, phone lines are down, and almost every stream is overflowing."

"You mean up in Virginia?" Mary Sue asked.

"That's right, Honey; they say that everything that isn't securely anchored is being washed away."

"Oh, no!" Mary Sue sighed. "Our home is on the banks of the Clinch River! Mom, Granny, and our little brothers are there by themselves. When is it supposed to stop raining?"

"Not until tomorrow night, I hear." Mama could see lines of worry and frustration forming on the faces of the two young ladies.

She walked to the wall phone to make sure the lines were still down. She poured a coffee for herself and sat down at their table. "I'm sure they will be alright," she said, trying as best as she could to console them.

They finished their stew and waited for some time for the storm to let up, but it only became more intense. It was only late afternoon, but the fog was so thick it might as well have been midnight. They were scared to get back on the highway and more afraid not to go. They thanked Mama, who had refused to let them pay for their food, and headed back out into the storm. They were about four hours from home if the weather had been nice but they knew they would be lucky if they could make it by midnight.

They had driven about an hour when J.D. decided he could not go any further. He pulled to within inches of the rear bumper of his daddy's pickup and waited for a slight break in the fog.

When at last he could see a few feet in front of them he gunned the Dodge and sailed around. He drove a short distance further and both vehicles pulled to the side. They had no idea where they were but decided it was too dangerous to go on until the storm passed. Ida Mae and Mr. Hurd got into the Dodge and the four of them settled in for the night.

Sometime just before dawn the down-pouring rain began to subside. The lightning bolts were somewhat less furious and the rumble of thunder less intense. As the fog started to lift the front of a large cattle barn came into view. J.D. could not have picked a more suitable place to stop. The moment the ladies recognized it was a barn they made a dash for the door. It may not have had running water but to a couple of country girls it was a welcome sight.

Shortly after daylight they started moving again. It was still raining, but not nearly so hard. The storm made every appearance of beginning to move further to the east, away from the mountains. The aftermath of the storm was visible everywhere. Tree limbs and mudslides partially blocked the highway. Utility poles were down; roofs were blown away; meadow fields resembled lakes, and every stream was out of its bank. It was like nothing any of them had ever seen, and the thought of what might have happened along the Clinch was foremost in their minds.

Just before noon, they crossed the Russell County line about an hour from home. Contrary to what they had hoped the devastation left behind by the storm was no less. Soaked furniture was being dragged from homes; small groups of people assembled to give aid to their neighbors, and emergency vehicles were everywhere.

The closer they came to the Clinch, the more frightened the sisters became. When they reached the outskirts of Cleveland, their worst fears became a reality. Water was knee deep in the streets and all businesses, including the post office, were closed.

Two engines of an N & W freightliner sat idle on the tracks, their wheels partially under water. A pickup truck floating on its side banged against one of the engines. Garden tools, children's toys, boards torn from houses, and a small building were moving rapidly downstream. The road along the tracks was impassable.

"Please come with us, J.D." Mary Sue pleaded as she and Ida Mae leaped from the vehicles and headed along the ridge that lay above the tracks. When they came in sight of the house their hearts almost stopped. The entire roof had been blown off and parts of it lay beside the tracks. The remainder was floating somewhere down the Clinch.

They started running as fast as their legs would carry them. J.D. overtook the girls and reached the dwelling first. He instructed them to stay outside as he leaped onto what remained of the front porch and forced the door opened. He searched through every room until he was satisfied there was no one inside.

"They've made it out," he yelled.

Relief and panic began tearing at every fiber of their being: Relief at not finding the family dead or badly injured, but fearful they may have tried to escape during the night and been swept down stream.

They rushed back to town and started searching for anyone who might know their whereabouts. J.D. sent his daddy on to Buchanan but would not hear of leaving the ladies by themselves. To try to use the telephones was out of the question. The only alternative was to search door to door. They spent hours visiting every home on the north side of the river, but no one had seen Mary Ellen, Granny, or either of the twins. They needed to cross to the other side, but the muddy water gushing over the only bridge made it impossible. They must wait for the water to recede or travel some thirty miles to the nearest bridge that would be far enough above the water to allow them to cross. It would be dark before they could make the trip to the other bridge and back down to the other side so they decided it would be best to wait.

J.D. parked his Dodge near the end of the bridge where they could see for nearly quarter mile upstream. They watched people's most prized possessions float down the river as they waited for the water to recede into its banks. Just before nightfall a large building came into view. If bobbled up and down and spun around just before crashing into the side of the bridge. The splinters of what was once the Caney Creek Baptist Church floated into history.

By dark, it was clear that being able to cross the bridge was some time away so the trio prepared to spend their second night in the Dodge. J.D. stretched out in the front and the ladies curled up in the back seat. Around midnight a police cruiser with a flashing red light pulled along side. Deputy Howard Barton exited the cruiser and asked if they were okay.

"We're okay," Mary Sue, answered "Do you know anything about Mom, Granny, and the boys?"

Howard dropped his head and spoke in a low gentle voice. "I hardly know how to tell you all, but they are the only people in the area not accounted for. A lady across the river saw them running from their house around noon yesterday, just as the roof blew off, but nobody has seen any of them since. If they're not found, we'll start searching downstream in the morning."

The sisters embraced each other and fought to hold back their tears. Mary Sue had never before felt so close to her older sister. They talked the remainder of the night away and listened to J.D. assure them that their family was going to be okay.

Just as it was breaking daylight, the fog started to lift; and the floor of the bridge came into view. It was too early to know if is was safe enough to drive across, but Mary Sue walked to almost the middle. She folded her arms along the top of the railing and stared at the rushing river beneath her feet.

"Don't jump, Sis, you'll get wet," she heard someone call out.

Her heart started beating so fast she felt it would jump out of her body. The twins came running along either side of the tracks and Mary Ellen and Granny were strolling hand in hand between the rails.

Howard arrived just in time to see the foursome emerge from out of the fog. He sounded three loud blasts with his siren, a signal to let everyone know they'd been found.

"Where have you been?" Mary Sue asked.

"Well, I've been promising my friend Gertie I would come visit her; and when the top blew off the house, I decided it would be as good a time as any."

"How come they didn't put you in jail, Sis?" Kevin asked.

"Because the judge said I was too pretty to be locked up."

"He lied," Kervin joked.

The girls were so happy to see their family unharmed nothing else mattered at the moment. "This is going to be a good day after all," Ida Mae exclaimed.

"More than you know," Howard added, as he winked at Mary Ellen and Granny.

Granny moved a little to the deputy, turned away from the others and whispered, "You've still got the tape, don't you, Buddy?"

"You betcha, and I made a cop . . . I'll tell you about it later."

Chapter Fifteen

A NEW BEGINNING

Phone lines were down, roads were blocked or badly damaged and bridges washed away but still the news of the devastation in the southern end of the county traveled rapidly. By midmorning, the streets in town were becoming crowded with people gathering to help those who lived along the river. Deputy Barton took charge of the volunteers; and in a short time, the task of cleaning up began to take place.

Men who owned pick-up trucks or farm tractors with wagons hauled load after load of debris from the railroad tracks and away from store fronts. Soaking wet garments were hung to dry on clotheslines, wire fences, tree limbs, or anything else strong enough to bear the weight. A huge mound of metal items, ready to be hauled to the scrap yard, lay beside the tracks; and damaged wooden furniture was hauled to the edge of town and piled in heaps to be torched later. The small town of Cleveland was taking on a new look.

Granny, Mary Ellen, and Ida Mae worked feverishly throughout the day. Mary Sue and the twins were further down river helping others in need. They were so busy helping their neighbors; they hardly had time to think of their own homeless situation. They assumed most all their belonging had been destroyed by the rising water or had been blown away, but their lives had been spared. Gertie's home was large enough to furnish them temporary shelter, and the storm had passed, so that was enough to outweigh the loss of their meager possessions.

Throughout the day people brought much needed supplies. Even strangers to the area brought clothing, blankets, small pieces of furniture and prepared food donated by out-of-town restaurants. They also brought news of other areas along the Clinch that had suffered equally as bad. Fortunately, there had been no deaths reported so, in the midst of all that had happened, folks found cause to rejoice.

Near sundown small groups of tired aching bodies began leaving for their own homes. Mary Ellen sat on the bench where she sat every Friday evening while waiting for Ira to come home. It was only midweek but she wished it to be Friday because she had never known a time when she needed him more than she did at that moment. In spite of all that had taken place, she needed his reassurance that everything would be all right.

She watched as shadows covered the street that ran through the center of town. She could see Granny and Ida Mae seated on the curb across the way, eating sandwiches, drinking soda pop and chatting like a couple of teenagers. Further down the street near the end of the bridge sat J.D.'s Dodge, but she remembered she had not seen him all day; nor had she seen Mary Sue or the twins.

Deputy Barton came to where she was sitting. His wet mud splattered uniform reminded her more of a ditch digger than a law enforcement officer. "Ready to go home, I'm sorry, I mean to Gertie's Mary Ellen?"

"Right away," she said and patted the seat beside her. "Please sit down and tell me what you have decided to do about Baxter."

The deputy looked in both directions to make sure no one else could hear what he was about to tell her. "It's in the hands of the prosecuting attorney," he told her in a voice that was barely above that of a whisper. "He has listened to the tape several times to make sure it was the sheriff who initiated the conversation, not that he ever had any doubts, mind you."

"Where is Baxter now?"

"Who knows?"

"Does he know about the tape?"

"Nothing. The prosecutor wants me to bring you and Granny to his office first thing Friday morning. He wants to interview the two of you before he takes this matter before the judge."

"The judge? Friday morning? That's day after tomorrow! Can't we wait until Ira is home?"

"I'm afraid not; this is a serious offense and the prosecutor wants it handled at once. Not only did he make improper advances toward you while on duty no less, he is also guilty of blackmail."

"Friday morning, we'll be ready. Will you take us to Gertie's now, Howard?"

"You know it; let's round up Granny and Ida Mae."

When all three ladies were in the cruiser Howard drove slowly along the rutted road beside the tracks. When he reached the remains of what had once been her home Mary Ellen asked him to stop. Several deep tire tracks indicated vehicles had been there during the day. She jumped from the cruiser and made her way up to the back of the house. When she looked inside, she was shocked beyond belief. Every room was bare! Someone had taken everything; only the floor, the walls, and part of the roof remained. She slowly made her way back to the cruiser. "We've been robbed, but I guess whoever did this awful thing must have needed it badly."

"Don't you worry; I'll take care of it immediately," Howard assured her.

He drove half-mile further along the tracks to Gertie's place. Gertie was sitting on her front porch in a straight-back chair, arms crossed, leaning against the wall. Mary Sue, J.D., and the twins were sitting on one of the rails acting like the cats that ate the canary.

It didn't take long for Mary Ellen to decide something out of the ordinary was going on. "Okay, what have all you been up to?" she asked.

The twins could not wait to let their mother know what was going on. "Come with us before it gets too dark, and we'll show you" Kervin exclaimed. Mary Ellen followed them to the large vacant barn that stood a distance behind Gertie's house. The same tire tracks that led from her dilapidated home ran beside Gertie's house toward the barn, so she guessed what had taken place. When the twins swung the big double barn doors open she got the surprise of her life. Every garment they owned was on hangers neatly separated on a pipe in front of one of the stalls. Pieces of furniture that had been thoroughly cleaned were placed on boards along the walls. Curtains hung on nails and two large laundry tubs were partially hidden; one contained undergarments and the other was filled with personal items that needed only Mary Ellen's attention.

Mary Ellen could hardly speak. "Thanks to all of you," she whispered. "You knew all about this?" she asked Howard.

"I told you. I'd take care of it immediately, didn't I?"

"I love all of you, and you're not all bad either, J.D."

"He is if he don't let me drive the Green Dragon again," Mary Sue cried out as she gave him a big hug. "Thanks, J.D., we couldn't have done all this without you."

"You ain't gettin' in my car with that mud all over you," he smiled. "But you have to know I am truly sorry for the trouble I caused you." He left later that evening for his parent's home over in the next county.

* * * * *

The rest of the family spent the next day helping friends and neighbors while Mary Ellen and Granny rested and made preparations for their trip to the prosecutor's office. Gertie knew they had to take care of some legal business, but she assumed it was something concerning the flood. Only Mary Sue and Ida Mae knew the real reason for their trip. Their mother told them the evening before but only after having them promise to keep it a secret.

Both ladies were up before sunrise on Friday morning. Granny remained calm, but Mary Ellen walked the floor until she saw Deputy Barton's cruiser come into view. She was hopeful Baxter would be severely reprimanded, forced to apologize to Ira and return him to his position as deputy. She was so anxious to get the matter out in the open, the trip to the County Seat seemed to take forever.

Granny, on the other hand, was enjoying the ride. She had never had the opportunity to ride in a police car before, and she was making the most of the trip. Mary Ellen was thankful they didn't see anyone they knew because Granny was waving at everyone they passed.

Howard pulled to the door of the prosecutor's office, let the ladies get out then parked the cruiser further down the street. He didn't want to have to explain to anyone why he had brought the ladies into town.

The attorney greeted the ladies with a handshake. He asked them to take a seat and waited until Deputy Barton came into his office before playing the tape. When the tape ended he asked each of them to raise their right hand and swear the recording had not been altered in any way.

After each of the ladies had done as he had asked, he simply stated, "I'll take it from here." He was very cordial and very professional, but they could tell by his expression he was both disappointed and angry.

"Does that mean he will be held accountable?" Granny wanted to know.

"You may count on it. I've already requested a meeting with the judge this afternoon."

"Is that all you need from us?" Mary Ellen asked.

"It is."

"Then let's get back home and wait for Ira," she told Granny.

"I'm ready," Howard remarked.

They stepped onto the street right into the face of Sheriff Baxter. He was parked directly in front of the prosecutor's office with the window rolled down, pretending to be reading the morning newspaper. "Good morning, ladies; having some legal problems?" he asked.

He had drastically underestimated Granny's ability to think fast. She glanced at the deputy whose face was blood red and hastily interrupted as he started to speak.

"We sure are having legal problems," she blurted. "We almost got washed off the face of the earth; the wind blew the roof off our house, and some jerk stole everything that was left. But if you had been doing your job you would know that already! Take us back home Deputy."

The sheriff had nothing more to say. He watched as Howard escorted the ladies to his cruiser and helped Granny inside.

Chapter Sixteen

THE CONFRONTATION

axter burst into the prosecutor's office as soon as the deputy's car was out of sight. "What reason did Barton have to bring those ladies into your office?" He demanded.

"I don't remember our having an appointment today," the attorney said as he rewound the tape, took the reel from the spindle, and placed it in his top desk drawer. "And to answer your question, we'll discuss it at the proper time."

"Do they have any idea who it was that made off with their belongings?"

"Do they what?"

"Their household stuff, that's why they were" . . . suddenly he paused. He realized that was not at all the reason they were in the prosecutor's office.

All at once the wheels within his head started turning. What if by chance she had recorded their conversation the other day when he was down on the river? After all her daughter loved to sing, and he had heard she was going to perform in a talent show. If this was true he had to do something fast or he was doomed.

"Did that tape have anything to do with their visit?" He asked almost panic stricken.

"I just told you, we'll discuss it at the proper time."

"What's wrong with us discussing it right now?"

"Because I have an appointment with the judge, and I won't be late. If you'll excuse me," the attorney said as he locked his desk and ushered the sheriff out of his office.

"Barton," that's the answer the sheriff decided and he jumped into his squad car and headed for Cleveland. He did not want to overtake his deputy, but he wanted to confront him as soon as he took Mary Ellen and Granny back home. He drove just fast enough to get into town as his deputy turned down along the railroad tracks. He parked at the far end of the river bridge and waited for his return. When the deputy made his return, the sheriff pulled in front of the cruiser completely blocking any access to the highway. He lurched from his car and approached Barton with fire in his eyes.

"What do you think you're doing?" he demanded.

"About what?"

"Don't be coy with me! And don't forget who you're working for either!"

Barton pushed the driver's side door open and stepped outside. He stood at least four inches taller than the sheriff and out-weighted him by at least fifty pounds, so he did not fear for his safety. He knew the sheriff might take his job, but he wasn't stupid enough to take him on in a fistfight.

"I have no idea what you're talking about."

"I want to know the real reason for your trip to the prosecutor's office."

"You heard what the lady said, so I don't understand why you are so upset."

Baxter hesitated a moment before he said anything further. If he had jumped to the wrong conclusion, he was making a fool of himself; and if he were correct, he knew what he had to do.

"I'm sorry, Howard. I've had a few personal problems lately, and I guess I'm getting a little paranoid."

"Women problems?"

"You know it."

"Then I guess I understand why you're a little touchy," He lied.

Baxter was relieved when the dispatcher came on the radio with an important message. The report was that the recent storm had done extensive damage in many parts of the state of West Virginia. Mines in the Kimball and Keystone area were flooded, and some of the miners were trapped. All able bodied men are staying on the job, keeping pumps running until their fellow workers are outside.

All streams in the area were flooding, bridges were gone, and communication lines are down. The only means of staying in touch with the outside world is through police radios.

The sheriff acknowledged the report and signed off.

Both officers knew of at least half-dozen men who lived in Cleveland and worked in those mines. Their families had to be made aware of the disaster.

"Stay out until all the families have the news. I have other important matters to take care of," the sheriff told Barton as he headed back to his office.

Howard turned his cruiser and started driving slowly back to Gertie's place. This was going to be the most difficult task he had ever faced. He felt close to all the members of the Duncan family, but Ira was one of his best friends. The possibility of him being trapped in an underground mine being filled with water made his entire body tremble.

He stopped just short of his destination and sat for several moments trying to find the words he needed to say. After a while he simply gave up, there was no easy way to tell the family what they might be facing. And why had it become his responsibility? What was it that suddenly demanded Baxter's attention?

The deputy parked his cruiser and started walking toward the house as Mary Ellen came out the door. "Forget something?" she asked. "I was on my way to wait for Ira; but since you're here, will you give me a ride back to town?"

"Ira's not coming." The words were out of his mouth before he realized this was the worst possible way he could have broken the news.

"What?" She screamed. The panic in her voice brought everyone inside the house rushing outdoors.

Howard made a feeble attempt at telling them what had happened while trying to dispel their fears.

"Take me to the mines," she begged.

It took some time for the deputy to get everyone calmed down enough to explain that all roads to the mines were closed and that a trip to West Virginia would be in vain. "I must go tell the other families before I get off duty, but I promise I will stay by the police radio all night. If I hear anything, I'll come tell you at once."

He turned to leave just as the roar of the mufflers on J.D.'s Dodge broke the silence. A moment later the Green Dragon came into view. "We heard about the West Virginia flood a couple hours ago and I came to see if there is anything I can do," J.D explained.

"Will you stay with the family until you hear from me?"

"You can count on me, Sheriff," J.D. stated.

Howard managed a smile. "Boy! That sure sounded good."

Getting news to the families of the other miners didn't take long. Most of them lived in or near the outskirts of town.

When the most tiring day of his police career came to an end, Howard headed for home. He was greeted with a warm smile, a gentle hug, and a steaming hot meal. The wood-burning stove the missus had refused to let go was a blessing in disguise.

Howard and his wife Betty were very close. They had been married shortly after finishing high school, but were never able to have children. Betty was active in their local church and took care of her widowed father who lived nearby. Howard worked at a sawmill until the owner passed away and then, despite Betty's wishes, took the job as deputy sheriff. They always enjoyed each other's company during their evening meal, but this was the first time they had eaten by candlelight. "Let's not ever have electricity again," he teased.

"Suits me; now get some rest."

Howard pulled his cruiser up near the opened window of their bedroom, turned the police radio up loud and collapsed on his bed. The radio was his only means of communication; and if there was any news about the miners, he wanted to be among the first to know. He was too uptight to sleep and to exhausted to stay awake so he tossed and turned until dawn. When he did finally muster enough energy to pull himself out of bed he went to the cruiser and radioed the dispatcher.

"Any news from the miners over in West Virginia?" he asked when the dispatcher answered his page.

"Not a word, Howard. It's Saturday; I thought this was your day off."

"It is, anything happening in the county?"

"Not much, we're playing host to a couple of boozers. And, someone broke into the prosecutor's office last night, but the sheriff is taking care of that himself.

"I'll bet."

"Repeat, I don't think I understand."

"Disregard. I'll be close my radio all day. Let me know if there's news from Kimball."

Barton could not help but smile. Suddenly, he was aware of the important matter Baxter had to attend to the evening before. It was he who had broken into the attorney's office. And I bet he has stolen the copy of our tape, the deputy thought. If he only knew the original is locked in the trunk of my car.

* * * * *

The news of the disaster at the mines spread like wildfire. By late afternoon a large crowd of family members, friends, and sympathizers began gathering on the streets of Cleveland. The First Baptist Church near the north end of town was filled to overflowing. A carload of men from the community left early in the morning to offer assistance and gather more detailed information, but still the families knew nothing.

As darkness fell over the small river town, people began to light candles. In light of what was now happening the events of the last few days did not seem so important. People sang, prayed, and offered condolences while they waited for any news from the mining towns. Howard sat alone in his cruiser near the church. He was so exhausted he was struggling to stay awake and trying to listen to everything that was taking place. Shortly after midnight the anxiously awaited news filled the air.

"Howard. Are you in your cruiser? If so, what is your twenty?"

The deputy was more asleep than awake, but the urgency in the dispatcher's voice brought him to attention.

"Ten-four, I'm in the cruiser; and I'm in Cleveland."

"Tell everyone the miners are outside, and they are all okay."

Howard turned on the loudspeakers to the maximum volume setting and placed the mike near the radio. "You tell them," he said and his voice almost cracked.

"May I have your attention, please? The miners are out and they are all safe." The message echoed through the streets. He repeated the message as candles were waved and shouts of joy became so loud they could have been heard a mile away.

Howard turned off the speakers and listened to further details. Although no one was injured, the miners chose to stay on the job until the water was pumped from the mines. "Let their families know they will be home as usual next Friday."

"Ten-Four."

"Oh, one more thing" the dispatcher added, "the judge wants to see you and the prosecutor in his chambers at nine o'clock sharp Monday morning."

Chapter Seventeen

A CALL TO JUSTICE

Howard arrived at the courthouse a half-hour before time for the appointment. He, like everyone else, knew the judge had no tolerance for tardiness so he was not about to be late. The prosecutor was early, also; but he was anything but happy. He was pacing the floor in the hallway outside the door to the judge's chambers. As quickly as he saw Howard, he came rushing to him. Howard had known the attorney for a long time and he had never seen him this upset about anything.

"We've got a problem, Deputy."

"We do?"

"Yes, we do! Someone broke into my office late Saturday night and stole the tape."

"They did?"

"I've tried to call you several times, but the phone lines are down. I explained this matter to the judge as soon as you left my office the other day. He advised me that this is a serious charge and that I had better have all my ducks in a row before he confronts the sheriff."

"What else did they steal, from your office, I mean?"

"Nothing of any importance, but what has that to do with anything?"

"Wonder who would want to steal nothing except the tape?"

"You and I both know who stole the tape, but try to tell that to the judge."

"You should have made a copy,"

"Now, you tell me! Why didn't you make a copy?"

"I did, but I've always wondered how I would feel to see you sweat," Howard said jokingly.

"Well, now you know, you son-of-a-gun. Where is the copy of the tape?"

"I believe Baxter has it, but the original is in the trunk of my car."

"I owe you a steak dinner when this is over," the prosecutor said as he breathed a sigh of relief. "If I had been unable to produce that tape, the judge would nail my hide to the courthouse door. Now, go get the tape, we can't keep His Honor waiting."

The judge listened to the tape; three times before he made any comment. Each time he looked more bewildered than the time before. Baxter's reputation had not escaped the ears of the judge, but he could not believe a man in his position would commit such an act.

The judge sat in silence shaking his head. "How many people know about this incident?" He asked.

"Deputy Barton, Ira's wife, his mother, and me, Your Honor."

"Where is the Sheriff now?"

"I have no idea, sir."

"Tell him I want to . . . Never mind, I'll do it myself. I'll need a couple days to consider what course of action I should take. I want to see both of you here in my chambers at ten o'clock Thursday morning. Bring the two ladies with you, and not a word of this to anyone."

The two men left the courthouse and headed for the prosecutor's office. "Well, what do you think?" The attorney asked.

"I think I'd really prefer a nice thick sirloin."

"I mean about—uh oh, look who's coming up the street."

Baxter had just rounded the corner and was headed straight toward them.

"Good morning gentlemen, what's up?" he asked.

The deputy was pleased when the attorney had a quick answer. "I was just giving Howard the low down about the breaking and entering at my office. Have you gotten any leads Sheriff?"

Baxter gave his deputy a distrusting gaze. "No, but I'm working on it. Have you made a list of everything that was taken?"

"I've really been busy, but I'll have it in a day or so."

"Swell, I'm handling this case personally. Let me know as soon as you have the list ready," Baxter snapped.

Howard went about his daily duties, but the sheriff was never far away. It was evident Baxter was determined to know his every move. He was careful not to go anywhere near Cleveland or back to the prosecutor's office while on duty. He needed desperately to get word to Mary Ellen and Granny about Thursday's meeting, but he was afraid he was being watched. Then out of the blue he was presented with a golden opportunity. He was parked at the edge of town when J.D's Dodge went roaring past. He immediately began pursuit and pulled him over. "How is everyone at Gertie's?" he asked.

"Hungry, I'm on my way to the grocery store, a lot of mouths to feed you know. Other than that, they're doing fine. When they learned Ira was safe, everyone settled down; but they are anxious for him to come home. What can I do for you, Howard? I'm sure I wasn't speeding."

"You'll have to trust me, Mr. Hurd."

"It's J.D. You only need to call me Mr. Hurd if you are going to put the cuffs on."

"All right, J.D., I need you to do me a favor."

Howard explained the urgent need to have Mary Ellen and Granny at the County Seat at the appointed time. "Just do it please, and don't ask any questions. I'll fill you in on all the details later."

"Consider it done, Deputy. Are you sure I wasn't speeding?" The words were barely out of his mouth when Baxter came cruising by.

"As a matter of fact you were, may I see your driver's license." Howard issued a ticket for speeding along with his personal guarantee that the charge would be dismissed. He placed his ticket book on the seat beside him where it could be clearly seen and watched J.D. drive off. He sat for a moment in anticipation of the sheriff driving past once again. He had him figured to a tee. Less than a minute later Baxter pulled his cruiser behind his own.

"What was that all about?" He asked as he walked up along side his deputy's car?

"Speeding," Howard reached for his ticket book.

"Yeah, Right."

Baxter marched back to his cruiser, slammed the door and took off with the rear tires smoking. It was evident he knew something was taking place. Not knowing was eating him alive.

Howard sailed through his duties the next two days with a breeze. He made a point to stay clear of his boss, but he could hardly wait to learn what would happen when they went back to visit the judge.

* * * * *

Deputy Barton was up early on Thursday morning in anticipation of an eventful day. He had no idea what the judge had in mind for the sheriff, but he knew he would be severely reprimanded, at best; and Howard was going to enjoy every minute of it. He just wished his buddy, Ira, could be there to watch his former boss squirm.

He waited outside the courthouse for Mary Ellen and Granny to arrive. At ten o'clock on the dot, J.D. pulled the Green Dragon up to where he was waiting. Barton ushered the ladies inside and instructed J.D. to get the Dodge out of sight until noon. The judge met them as they came inside and showed them to his private office.

The judge was dressed in a pair of blue jeans and a short-sleeved shirt and a pair of grass-stained tennis shoes. He was as informal and friendly as if he were the neighbor who lived next door. They drank coffee and ate donuts while the he questioned the ladies about what led up to the visit by the sheriff the day the recording was made. When he was satisfied he had all the information he needed, he told them what was to happen next.

"I've requested the sheriff to be in the courtroom at exactly eleven o'clock. Only he and those of us who are in this room will be present. I will confront him about his unprofessional conduct and listen to his comments. I ask that you remain silent unless I find it necessary to question you myself." He covered his informal attire with a black robe and led them into the courtroom.

The judge chatted with Mary Ellen and Granny about the results of the flood, Ira's well being and various other topics while he watched the hands on the large courtroom clock. At a quarter past the hour he was quite noticeably becoming impatient. Howard began to gloat, for he knew this was not going to sit well with the judge. But he also knew the sheriff was intentionally being somewhat belligerent, just displaying a portion of his own authority. But he was quite confident the judge would need only a moment to remind him who was in charge.

The deputy was right in his thinking. At twenty minutes after the hour, Baxter came waltzing into the courtroom. It took only a moment for him to determine he might be in a compromising situation, but his demeanor did not change.

" Why, good morning ladies, I'm sorry about your loss due to the flood. I should have been by to see you, but I was busy in other areas of the county. And, I'm sorry I found it necessary to dismiss Ira, but I was forced to protect the integrity of my office, **you understand.** Good morning to you Your Honor."

"Sit down and shut up," the judge shouted, "or I'll find you in contempt."

"I'm sorry, Your Honor; I didn't know court was in session."

146

"It will be, if necessary," he said as he gave one sharp rap with his gavel.

Baxter sank into a chair like a whipped pup. What's this all about?" he questioned.

"Will you read the pending charges?" the judge asked the prosecutor.

"Certainly, Your Honor," the attorney stated with enthusiasm. "Mrs. Mary Ellen Duncan alleges that the sheriff, William Baxter, made an uninvited visit to her home. And, that while believing she was alone, made advances toward her."

"That's a lie," Baxter roared.

"Quiet," the judge ordered.

"He also," the prosecutor continued, "promised special favors to her and her family if she agreed to do as he asked. That, Your Honor, is nothing less than blackmail. And without knowing it, he did so in the presence of a witness."

Baxter jumped to his feet. "That's preposterous, Your Honor; not a word of these accusations are true. I would never do such a thing. They can't prove anything they're saying."

"May I continue, Your Honor?"

"You may."

The prosecutor walked to a small table in front of the judge's bench. He removed the cloth cover from a tape recorder and started the reel turning.

Baxter's face turned the color of chalk.

"What were you saying about being able to prove these accusations, Sheriff?"

"I think I may need an attorney."

"You certainly may, but let me give you a bit of food for thought," the judge stated. "At this time there have been no formal charges brought against you, only because Mrs. Duncan chose to handle it in this manner. You may resign, effective immediately, giving whatever reasons you choose, in order to save yourself a great deal of embarrassment. And, you can never be employed in law enforcement ever again. Or, I will exercise my authority to place you on suspension until you have ample time to hire an attorney and face charges in open court. If you choose the former, I will issue a gag order, and what took place here today never happened. I will extend you the undue courtesy of having until five o'clock to give me your answer. And that doesn't mean twenty minutes after!" he added.

"I don't need any favors or your twenty minutes either! I quit!" Baxter said as he removed his badge and laid it on the table in front of him. "I'll leave the remainder of my equipment in my office, I mean over at the jail. Am I free to leave?"

"You are."

Baxter turned and started toward the exit at the back of the courtroom. As he passed Mary Ellen she smiled and said, "I had to do what I had to do, **but you do understand.**"

The judge waited until Baxter was out of the courtroom. "Now, it becomes my duty to appoint an acting sheriff to serve until the end of Baxter's term or until we can organize a special election. I can't think of anyone more qualified at the moment than you, Deputy Barton."

"I'm honored sir; but with all due respect, I would like to recommend Ira Duncan be given that position.

"Then so be it. Man, it's hot in here," the judge said as he unzipped his robe and hung it on the back of his chair. "You are a mighty brave lady, Mary Ellen; and I'm confident Ira will make an excellent sheriff."

"May I ask a favor, Your Honor?"

"You certainly may."

"Would it be okay if Howard, I mean Deputy Barton, takes us to West Virginia to get Ira?"

"Yes, ma'am, after all, that is official business."

CHAPTER EIGHTEEN

NEW OCCUPATION

Mary Ellen wasn't about to waste another minute getting her man back to where he belonged. As quickly as her foot touched the sidewalk, she asked Howard if he were ready to leave for West Virginia.

"As soon as I go home and tell Betty the news, we'll be on our way. If we're lucky, we'll be in Kimball before dark."

"Take me to Gertie's and pick up the girls; it's only fitting they should go," Granny insisted.

"You're a doll, Mother Duncan. That's mighty kind of you."

Granny squeezed her daughter-in-law's hand; those were the kindest words she'd heard in years. "How could I have ever mistrusted you?" she whispered.

Mary Ellen turned away as Granny blinked rapidly to fight back a tear. She had, after so many years, pierced the protective armor of the Duncan family matriarch.

It was later than they had anticipated when Deputy Barton, Mary Ellen and the girls left Cleveland to begin the long trip into the mining town of West Virginia. It wasn't the miles that ate away at Mary Ellen's patience; it was the time it took to get there. She knew Ira's shift underground would be over, and she was determined to get there in time to make sure it was to be his last.

Suddenly, she was overcome by the thought of what she might find. The rumors about what went on in the boarding houses of some of the small mining towns began to make her uneasy. What if she found Ira indulging in some activity unsuited for a family man? The decision to bring her daughters along might not have been such a good idea. She began talking of anything that came to mind in order to dispel these unsavory thoughts; but she became a little more nervous as the miles rolled by.

It was almost dark when they crossed the mountaintop near the state line. As they descended into the valleys where most of the coal mines were located evidence of the flood was everywhere. Electricity had not yet been restored and it was pitch black. The headlights from the cruiser did little to pierce the darkness. Numerous mudslides and downed trees still made some of the highway almost impassable.

Half an hour later a road sign, identifying Keystone, which was their destination, came into view. Rows of houses blackened with coal dust lined the street. Mary Ellen was sure that daylight would make the town appear less depressing, but she suddenly developed a greater appreciation for farm living.

The faint glow of candlelight was occasionally visible through the windows of the row houses, but most seemed completely deserted. To Mary Ellen and the girls the place was so eerie it might as well been a ghost town. But, when they reached the center of the settlement, the atmosphere drastically changed. At least half-dozen establishments were bursting with excitement. Oil lamps lined the front edges of the porches and hung on either side of open doorways. Loud piano music poured from each and pretty ladies in short skirts and low-cut blouses were dancing with or serving drinks to their patrons.

Howard parked the police cruiser a short distance from the nearest place of entertainment and suggested the ladies remain in the car. As he approached the first barroom, he wished he'd had the foresight to change clothes. Too late now, he surmised, as he stepped inside.

"Well, if it ain't Wyatt Earp," one of the barmaids yelled as she pranced in front of him with a tray filled with drinks. "I don't know what you're after, but I'll be right back to get it for you," she laughed.

"Just information. I'm looking for some one," the deputy informed her.

"No kidding, what's her name."

"Ira, Ira Duncan, ma'am"

"Now ain't that a strange name for a lady," she giggled.

"I guess. Have you seen him?"

"Never heard of him."

"I know him," an elderly miner told him, "work with him every day. He lives at the last boarding house at the end of the street; good worker, but keeps pretty much to himself when we're not in the mines."

Howard walked back to the cruiser and drove slowly toward the building the old gentleman described. They were out of sight of the action, and the street was dark once more. The only sign of life was that of a miner who sat alone on the porch of a boarding house. The light from his mining helmet illuminated the writing pad that lay on his lap and the pencil that had almost slipped from his fingers. Howard turned off the engine and drifted up to where the miner seemed to be napping.

"Excuse me sir, could you tell me . . . ?"

The coal black miner raised his head and Mary Ellen leaped from the cruiser. She threw her arms around Ira and her tears began leaving streaks on his coal-blackened face.

"What are you doing here? Has something bad happened at home?"

"Quite the contrary, Sheriff, we've come to take you home. "Mary Ellen smiled at him.

They were so excited they kept interrupting each other as they told Ira all that had happened since he left Cleveland.

"Let me take a bath, and we'll be on our way."

"Not on your life; gather your belongings; you can bathe in the Clinch when you get home," Mary Ellen teased.

Ira rushed upstairs to his room, grabbed his lunch pail, a small bundle of clothing and left Keystone for the last time.

The trip back home was a journey to remember. It was difficult to tell who was the most excited. It was truly a time for celebration, and to add to their good fortune when they rolled into Cleveland, the streets lights were burning.

They stopped by the tracks in front of Gertie's just as the sun came up. Everyone was up, dressed, and waiting to welcome Ira home. J.D., who had stayed to take care of Gertie, Granny, and the twins was about to leave for home.

"Give me the keys to The Dragon," Mary Sue told him.

"Not a chance! Remember what happened the last time I let you drive."

"Yes, but this time I'm going to see what's in the trunk." She playfully wrestled the his keys from his hand, raised the deck lid, and retrieved the new clothing she'd bought for her family while she was in Winston.

"We'll need these Monday when our new Sheriff is sworn in. Will you be there?"

"With bells on!"

Chapter Nineteen

ANOTHER REUNION

Jake also arrived in time to witness Ira taking the oath of office. He had some exciting news of his own which would add to the day of celebration.

"I've enrolled you in one of the best high schools in Winston Salem," he told Mary Sue. "And if you wish, you can perform with Eddie Mayfield and his band every weekend until graduation."

Mary Sue could hardly believe her ears. At last she would be fulfilling her dreams while living *In Her Sister's Shadow.*

Ira spent the next few days with his newly appointed chief deputy Howard Barton catching up on the legal matters. Jake and the females in the Duncan family spent their time finding a new place to live.

Ira purchased a home not far from the Baxter farm so Mary Ellen, Granny, and the twins felt right at home. The ladies talked to Ida Mae almost every day on their newly installed telephone, and Mary Sue was making preparation for her move to Winston.

John Robert also called at least once a week. He promised a surprise when he came home, but would never reveal his secret.

The twins spent their days roaming the mountain in search of ginseng or other herbs or earning a few dollars working on neighboring farms.

Granny rejoined her Ladies Group and did more than her part to help spread the local gossip. She also pitched in with every task Mary Ellen started; in her own way, she was repenting for past resentment.

Baxter sold his cattle, leased his farm, and moved to parts unknown—for health reason, he explained. There were as many stories about his leaving as there were hot days of summer; but by fall, the rumors had all but ceased. The once quiet peaceful setting of the county had again returned.

J.D. convinced his moonshine acquaintances it would be more profitable to work for his daddy in the logging business than to try to haul their product out of the county. As a result, his father became one of the largest lumber suppliers for miles around. J.D. visited the Duncans as often as time would allow; he, too, was anxious to move to the Carolinas to begin his career in auto racing. He began to show special interest in Mary Sue; but each time she felt he was about to ask her out, she reminded him that her education would come before dating. She did, however, promise that when he was on the track she would be leading his cheering section.

The hot days of summer gave way to fall; and Mary Sue's dreams were becoming a reality. She'd moved to Chestnut Street and was taking advantage of every adventure offered by a big city. She made numerous friends at school, and her grades were near the top in her senior class. Most every weekday night was spent in her studies, but the weekends found her on stage. She was becoming well-known in some of the best entertainment spots in the city of Winston.

As the Thanksgiving holiday season approached, Mary Ellen, Granny, and the twins began making plans for their family reunion. The telephone calls home became more frequent, and the excitement was mounting. The forthcoming surprise John Robert promised made the day seem even more eventful. Mary Sue was bringing good news, and Granny had a surprise of her own. The men folk were so excited about all the family being together, they even cancelled their annual hunting excursion.

* * * * *

Thanksgiving morning could not have been more perfect. The early rays of sunlight burned away the last traces of fog, and there was not a cloud in the sky. The aroma of freshly baked pumpkin pies cooling on a windowsill filled the air.

The twins piled sand around horseshoe pegs in preparation for part of the holiday weekend entertainment. Ira was off somewhere running an errand for Granny, while she and Mary Ellen added the final touch to the Thanksgiving feast. This task was constantly interrupted by trips to the front windows to see which of the siblings would arrive first. By midmorning, these trips became unnecessary. As if on cue, Jake, Ida Mae, and Mary Sue pulled to the side of the road near the front gate. John Robert and a beautiful young lady followed close behind in a brand new Chevrolet.

The new arrivals had barely had time to say hello when Ira's cruiser came into view. A sharp blast of his siren was his way of saying welcome home. "That was Gertie's idea," he said as he helped Granny's surprise out of the car.

"I sure hope you don't mind me inviting Gertie," Granny whispered to Mary Ellen. "She has no family, and I couldn't stand to have her spend Thanksgiving alone."

Mary Ellen placed her arm around Granny's shoulder and pulled her close. "I wish I'd thought of that."

John Robert opened the passenger side door of the Chevy and a gorgeous brunette stepped outside. "I'd like all of you to meet my fiancée, Miss Susan Webb," he said. His announcement was met with kind greetings, applause, and wide eyes. Her peachy complexion made her long brown hair look even more stunning and the lace atop her emerald green dress matched the pearls that hung loosely about her slender neck.

"Hi, You're something to look at," Kervin chimed. "I never figured our big brother to marry a lady from the city."

"I did grow up in the center of downtown Grundy," she smiled.

"That's just across the mountain, near where Jake and J.D. grew up. Kervin, you talk too much," Kevin reminded him.

"You're right," John Robert told him. "Susan graduated high school and moved to the coast to find employment. I met her in a coffee shop near the shipyard where we both work."

The family ate, laughed, danced, sang, played games, and frolicked far into the night. As the clock struck midnight the older members began to get tired. "Bedtime," Granny yelled, "but only if you promise to start again in the morning."

Susan, Ida Mae, and Mary Sue shared one bedroom, Jake and the twins another, and Gertie bunked in with Granny. The older folks might just have well stayed up, for laughter from the young folks' bedrooms could be heard until almost dawn.

Their late breakfast the next day consisted of leftovers from their Thanksgiving dinner, but no one objected. It only served to give them more time to visit before they began their journeys back home.

They talked of all the good and bad times that had taken place since the last reunion day. They spoke of the damage caused by the flood and how grateful they were Gertie had shared her home. They talked about the events leading up to Baxter's downfall and Ira's fear of working the mines. They talked of Mary Sue's pending career as an attorney and her success on stage. And just before making preparations to leave they talked of Mary Sue's trial.

"How did you manage to avoid jail time?" Susan asked.

"I guess I just made a good impression on Old Judge Duff," Mary Sue told her.

"Who?" Granny questioned.

"Judge Duff."

"Where's he from, you know?"

"Have no idea."

"Do you know his first name or anything about him?"

"Sidney, I think," Jake interjected. "Yeah, I'm sure attorney Wallace said his first name was Sidney. He's quite wealthy, retired, been widowed for some time and fills in on the bench if the need arises."

Well it has been fun, but it's time for us to leave," he concluded.

"Just a minute," Granny said and disappeared into her room. Right away she reappeared with suitcase in hand.

"Where you going, Mom?" Ira asked.

"To North Carolina! Sidney was my first boyfriend, even asked me to marry him. I would have, too, if he hadn't got caught running shine over in the next county. Cut out before he went to trial, and I haven't heard from him since."

The End

080317